DALREAGH: Castle, Chapel, Crypt

Its mistress: A somnambulist passionately loved, recently and mysteriously widowed.

Its master: Her brother-in-law. Too handsome. Too knowing.

Its legend: *The Black Abbess*—an erring nun who died for love and returned for spite centuries later. Death was her path. Fear was her wake.

When Anne Killain was summoned to Mist House by her grieving friend Lucie Fairbairn Dalreagh, she welcomed the opportunity to ease the memory of her own dead husband. But when she came to Dalreagh, Anne found a Lucie transformed by a baptism of fear, a Lucie who had become the living shadow of a secret too terrible to tell. Lucie had requested her to come for a very specific purpose. And even in her wildest dreams, Anne would never have suspected that her true duties as housekeeper would include scouring a sepulcher to unearth its secrets. . . .

The Mist at Darkness

by Virginia Coffman

A SIGNET BOOK from
NEW AMERICAN LIBRARY
TIMES MIRROR

SIGNET TRADEMARK REG. U.S. PAT. OFF. AND FOREIGN COUNTRIES
REGISTERED TRADEMARK—MARCA REGISTRADA
HECHO EN CHICAGO, U.S.A.

Signet, Signet Classics, Mentor, Plume and Meridian Books
are published by The New American Library, Inc.,
1301 Avenue of the Americas, New York, New York 10019

First Printing, September, 1968

7 8 9 10 11 12 13 14 15

PRINTED IN THE UNITED STATES OF AMERICA

For Truffles and Timmy,
For Tippy and Mortimer and
Tinker,
Semper Fidelis

1

Though I have been a scullery maid in my time, I chanced to marry a member of the French aristocracy; but after his death at war, I was obliged, not entirely happily, to return to domestic service. Through the aid, however, of my former employer, Miss Hunnicut, who runs a girls' school in London, I was able to gain a position which hopefully would prove only temporary and which would entail being a housekeeper for the family of a former student of Miss Hunnicut's, one Lucie, now a widow, though still young, and sister-in-law to Sir Richard Dalreagh, a lord in the North. Lucie's young husband, Kevin, brother to Sir Richard, had recently died, following an accident which had put him, I gathered, in a bad temper indeed for some few months prior to his death. Lucie's plea to Miss Hunnicut was a direct one for me, and though the Dalreagh estate was said to be haunted by an ancient Black Abbess, mistress to a former Lord Dalreagh, and Lucie was said to be much disturbed of late, given to sleepwalking and scenes, I accepted the offer.

The former housekeeper had been hastily sent packing, and it seemed that I might be useful to these people for a time. So it was that I found myself on the road North, traveling by coach, one winter's afternoon, in the year 1821.

Having taken particular pains to leave London at a proper hour on the public stage, I avoided the mail coach which would set me down at Dalreagh Dale crossroad shortly before midnight, an awkward time, indeed, in which to present myself to my employers. But if one thing could be sure in an unsure world, it was that the Accommodation Coach would be late, no matter when it set out. And so it was that we racketed northward during the sharp, chill, sunny winter's day, a full company of strangers, chiefly male, and growing fuller as the taprooms of all the inns along the route were passed.

By late afternoon, the boy who blew for the turnpikes and those unfortunate riders on the roof were swaying frantically as the top-heavy coach rattled around every turn on the high road, which itself grew more and more rutted, strewn with the debris of a recent storm. The coachman, however, as well fortified for any eventuality, having an apparently endless capacity for either Rum Fustian or Blue Ruin. He took every turn in the heavily wooded hills as though he had a wager on the outcome, and very likely, he had.

Two stout ladies with pronounced Lancashire accents were regaling the rest of us with their opinion of the coachman as we all fell against each other. A very youthful clergyman who had timidly hugged the corner seat since he entered at our noon stop, now lowered the window, apologizing to the ladies present, and peered out.

"Dear me," he murmured, "this is a very bad region for such speed. We are approaching the Dalreagh Forest."

I looked up quickly and glanced out of the window; not for long, as the ladies complained of the cold, but I was able to glimpse the heavily wooded region, which shut out the long twilight of the North, so that the only lights to show the way around these sharp curves were the coach lights themselves, hardly adequate to illuminate any more than the coach's length.

"Do call that monstrous creature to account!" one of the Lancashire ladies ordered the young clergyman in battle tones.

The clergyman cringed, coughed, and looked

around for help before the dreaded confrontation with a huge and burly coachman. The Lancashire woman then informed us all, knowingly, when she had picked herself off the clergyman, after a new and accidental assault resulting from the pitch of the coach, "This is not a safe region, you must know. They've had infamous popish plots here. Priests in hiding. Plots to set the Scottish Mary upon the throne of England. Scandalous doings. The Abbess of Blackford was starved to death hereabouts for her sins." She leaned closer to her friend, though her voice rang out for all to hear. "I daren't tell you what crime she committed, the black-hearted hussy! It concerned the *male sex* . . . the Earl of Dalreagh. Only, of course, the Dalreaghs were only viscounts then."

I remembered the tale of the Black Abbess, and seeing the delighted horror on the faces of the other passengers, all but the clergyman, I felt called upon to explain.

"Excuse me, ma'am. But that'll be some centuries gone by. Not involving the present earl nor his family."

General disappointment was evident, and the woman, feeling herself corrected, said triumphantly, "Nonetheless, the Dalreaghs have been accurst for centuries because of it. They die!"

I was about to make the obvious retort that

such a curse afflicted most of us, but her friend was already saying, "Tell, tell!"

And the rest of us, tired of the jolting, the bouncing, and the uneasiness of our immediate future, could not help being audience to her absurd talk.

"Well, my dear, scarcely a fortnight is gone since the present younger Dalreagh died. A very mysterious doing, from all accounts."

"How so, ma'am?" I asked, this time with genuine curiosity.

"But of course! It was given out that he died of a lung complaint. Why, then, did he have strong convulsions before death, exactly as if he had been—"

I had a nasty feeling the word "poison" was on her lips, but she seemed to show sudden discretion and say instead, "as if he had been stricken by the touch of that creature."

I could see even the downy-faced clergyman looking at her with eyes wide, and the other man, an elderly townsman, awoke from his attempted nap, rubbed his head where it had bumped against the frame of the coach window, and inquired a bit thickly,

"What creature, ma'am? Some young female?"

"In a sense. She was young once, the Abbess of Blackford Abbey, her that the ancient Dalreagh seduced."

The old man laughed jeeringly, and I caught

myself smiling, although the fact that such gossip could exist at all about a family like the Dalreaghs was not at all funny.

"You need not scoff," said the gossipy woman, obviously nettled. "The Dalreagh mansion itself is built on the site of the first Blackford Abbey. Even the Abbey Crypt is beneath the house, I'm told. You will allow that is running counter to fate."

She would have gone on with equal vigor, but two things happened, one being the quiet courage of the young clergyman, who reminded her that she was sacrilegious, and the other was the furious rattling of the team's harness, the sway of the coach violently to the right, and then a great bumping under us and a sharp drop, still on the right side.

We all piled over on the poor clergyman, realizing that one of the coach wheels must have broken off. The bundled men on the roof of the coach had miraculously escaped serious injury and were scrambling down now, some threatening to have the coachman jailed for a public danger and others to investigate the damage and make their suggestions for getting the unwieldy coach back on the road.

The Lancashire ladies were so angry with the coachman that they did not have time or inclination to be frightened. When we climbed out, they were still arguing vigorously with the elderly man. The young clergyman cheered a boy who had gotten a bruised arm that bled a great deal. While I bandaged his arm, using one of my handkerchiefs, the clergyman told the boy tales of the hero Robin Hood, pretending that Dalreagh Forest was the bandit's true home.

When I was finished, I went around to where the men were at work on the wheel by the lamplight, but the axle was cracked, and it all looked very discouraging to me. All the time, I knew that the carriage from Mist House that was to meet me must be close at hand, waiting now, if only I knew where it was in this world of wood-scented darkness.

The coachman, sobered by the disaster and nursing a bloody nose, had gone off on foot, with one of the passengers from the roof, headed for Dalreagh Dale, the nearest village. Another roof passenger, busily rolling up the sleeves of his greatcoat the better to work, looked up in a friendly way when I spoke.

"I am to be at Dalreagh Crossroads," I explained. "It is said to be south of the village. Is it far, do you think?"

"Keep to this road, Miss. Not far. Y'd make it inside half an hour, a fine, healthy figure of a lass like ye'rself. Y'ell know the place for the bridge hard by. All is limestone hereabouts, from the caves and the quarries, as ye may know. Dalreagh estate road follows the river to Mist House . . . Ye're no' afraid, then?"

I was very much afraid—that the carriage from Mist House would give up and return to the manor without me. I did not wish to spend the entire night wandering about. I much preferred the brisk walk along the open high road at this early hour. It still lacked four hours of midnight, so that, at the moment, I was not yet late. It had been presumed that I should reach the Crossroads between eight and nine of the evening.

"But is there danger on this road?" I asked. "I have not heard that highwaymen were operating hereabouts." I suppose I spoke this way out of my innocence, because I had several times found myself able to make defense against physical evil. In view of the conversation within the coach, I should have been better prepared for the man's curious warning.

"Highwaymen are no' busy upon yon road in winter. Too muddy by half. They canna' ride off fast-like, ye'll take my meaning. No, Miss, that's no' but what there'll be danger. Mark'ee, now."

It was growing later by the minute, and I glanced anxiously at the road ahead.

"I really must be going. Excuse me." I was also beginning to be depressed by the thought of walking along a muddy winter road in my good new morocco slippers. For the rest, I was fortunate to be wearing my green winter cloak and hood, which were adequate covering for most coach-road disasters, which, heaven knows, are common enough, even in summer.

I was already on my way when he called after me the uncomfortable thought, "Why d'ye fancy the coach went off so? 'Twas not for the coachman who'd had a drop. No, Miss. 'Twas the team, ye'll notice. They're that skittish he could not keep 'em to the road."

One of the Lancashire ladies came around to investigate the situation and particularly the team, which was behaving very nervously, with much snaffling, stamping, and a rattling of harness, despite the vigorous attentions of several male passengers.

"What set the team afrighted, I wonder?" asked the lady and then peered deep into the undergrowth, which seemed to reach out its still wet and dripping branches toward the team pair on the left side, closest to the woods.

I refused to speculate further on any weirdness that might have startled the team, for fear there should be a contagion in that behavior. The other passengers were still calling advice and warnings to me when I hurried off northward into that apparently endless tunnel of dripping greenery. Once on my way, despite the immediate splashing of my new slippers, I felt that my destination would soon be reached and I could get on with my task at hand, to put in order the household affairs of Lucie Dalreagh. It is curious, I think now, that I did not ask myself more about the riddle of the woman who had previously held my new post as housekeeper. Surely, by this time, she must have reported to her former employer, Mrs. Shane-Porter, whose social connections would gain her a new post. Well, the comings and goings of Rachel Herrenrath could not interest me long that night.

For some minutes, I walked very rapidly. Aside from the atmosphere, decidedly unsettling to the nerves, the icy chill of winter was in the air, and I felt much more comfortable, closely wrapped as I was in my woolen cloak, swinging along my old portmanteau, which bore my immediate necessities. But I missed the horsemen and hoofbeats, the carriages and their teams that gave human life to the usual high road. In their place, I was presently aware of the enormous vitality of nature, which was encroaching on me from both sides, thinking that sentient creatures seemed to know exactly who I was and what my destination was and were, perhaps, with their wavering toward me and then away from me, considering slyly whether to attack or not.

When I was perhaps halfway between the broken coach and the village of Dalreagh Dale, the extraordinary silence that seemed so noticeable after the rattle of the Accommodation Coach now gradually dissolved. I caught the moan of the winter wind among the wet leaves, carrying on it a powerful scent of sodden earth and moldering piles of leaves, which puzzled me by their presence this late in the season and despite the presence of that wind. But as I hurried along, I was aware of the many stones, rocks, and lime deposits scattered everywhere throughout the woods, and I realized that the piles of leaves must have been swept by the wind to the base of these rocks, so that even now they still swirled around in little maelstroms that, I confess, made me cry out stupidly when they wound about my feet, clutching at me, sticking to me, sealed against my cloak and even my face, cold, acrid, soggy, things, smelling of death.

The farther I went, the more my form became the target for the blown leaves, the dust, and, occasionally, the shower of raindrops. It was during one of these moments, when I was hurrying along very near what I supposed to be my destination, that I was again assailed by a blowing torrent of leaves and debris, which left me blinded for several seconds while I clawed the leaves away.

Opening my eyes after that brief period of darkness, I was much better able to see into the immense black of the deeper woods beyond the road. Within that darkness, which had many facets and shades, I was startled to see a tall woman or man in an unfashionably long cloak standing within the first deep shadow of a grove of oaks and watching me. So much underbrush had grown up between the fat, gnarled tree trunks that only half the watcher's body seemed to be visible to anyone passing on the road. As there was a definite break in the interlaced tunnel ahead, I felt sure I was close to my destination; this creature, so sinister in its silence and very presence, had likely been taking a shortcut across country from the village nearby.

I remained quite still for a minute, staring hard; for I could scarcely understand why any human being, if it was a human being, should choose to stand there watching me at this hour of night and in rain-soaked ground, unless for some sinister purpose. But I was delaying. As I stepped forward along the road, though, aware in an unconscious way of the muddy damp that encrusted my feet inside my slippers, I looked carefully at the watching figure within the woods, trying to tell myself there was some logical reason for its presence.

The opening in the tunnel of trees ahead of me suddenly revealed the stone bridge that I supposed must mark the river and the crossroads I had been told to expect. It was a welcome sight. But the opening itself allowed a high and tiny moon to shine down, and a few vagrant beams filtered through the edge of the woods so that the silent watcher became faintly silhouetted. I could not believe my first real sight of that form as it was illuminated. The clothing I had mistaken for a cloak appeared to be only part of a robe that covered the head as well. And then I thought I understood. What I saw was the black habit and coif of a nun.

Or an abbess?

I ran nearly to the limestone bridge in the distance before getting hold of my courage, horribly ashamed of such arrant cowardice. When I paused to catch my breath and to look back, feeling, despite the cold, quite hot with the knowledge of my shameful retreat, I was too far away from the strange figure to be sure that it was any more than a horrid fancy. I told myself now that I had conjured up the thing as a result of all the hints by my fellow coach passengers. The explanation brought me a measure of self-assurance so that I could walk calmly up on the bridge and study the brightly illuminated scene, where only the topmost branches of the hovering woods cast their shadows over the crossroads at the south approach.

I could hear neither hoofbeats nor the rattle of harness on the smaller, badly rutted trail following the riverbank west, which I assumed was the Dalreagh Estate road, and wondered in what case I should be if no one arrived. Still farther to the north, beyond the tree tops, I made out a church spire and assumed this was Dalreagh Dale. It, too, was a welcome sight, for I knew I might find accommodations there if all else failed me.

The roar of the wind was scarcely more than a sigh out here in the open freedom of the bridge. Wrapping myself more closely in my cloak, I settled myself on the thick wall of the bridge, removed my slippers one at a time and scraped off the mud against the roughened outcroppings of stone beside me. During this time, I became increasingly aware of the enormity of the advancing night around me and of the pervasive silence. Several times, I imagined I heard the welcome sounds of an approaching carriage on the estate road, but these proved mere fancies, like that preposterous Abbess I had conjured up some minutes earlier out of what was undoubtedly a tree trunk with a scattering of leaves that still clung to the branches.

Hearing again the sound of hoofbeats rapidly nearing from the direction of Mist House, I got down off the wall and began to walk back the few steps to the crossroads. I was now much closer to the outer reaches of Dalreagh Forest and cast an uneasy glance in that direction before looking hard in the westerly direction where the estate road twisted and turned, so that I could not see far enough to assure myself that I had not imagined this new sound.

A sharp sound, the break and then snap of a fallen branch underfoot, made me swing around quickly toward the forest. That black, monolithic thing was real. I caught just the end of a quick movement before all was still again, only the wind was moaning above us. The thing was playing a game with me, and surely . . . surely, it must be real. But how still it stood now, in the deep shadows! Again it appeared to be some stupid fancy of mine, hardly more than a straight, unyielding tree trunk . . .

2

Almost in these same seconds, the sounds of hoofbeats with the accompaniment of jangling harness came closer, and I tightened my grip on my portmanteau, starting across the road in a great rush. I kept glancing back over my shoulder as I hurried along the riverbank, hoping to intercept the Mist House coach. Curiously enough, the further I retreated from the high road, the safer I felt. (It is one of the oddities of fate that we sometimes rush to our destiny, for good or ill, in the very act which we believe carries us away from that destiny. So it was with the Abbess. I ran from her, only to run, in the end, into those deadly hands.)

Almost before I could jump out of the way, a great wheeled monster hurtled around a turn, with its team's flying hooves very near to running me down. There was no postilion, and the coachman himself was heavily bundled against the weather, so that I could scarcely see whether he was young or old, friendly or otherwise, when I hailed him. When he pulled up beyond me, just at the point where the high road crossed the bridge, I hurried back, retracing my steps and calling to him:

"Are you from Mist House, sir?"

The man nodded—a difficult task, for his head, neck, and throat were swathed in a huge plaid neckcloth. He leaped off his high box, let down the steps for me, and tossed in my portmanteau as I stepped in, relieved to be on the way to my final destination. It was stuffy in the coach, and I lowered the window, calling out, "I am ready, sir." The coachman merely looked around at me, his protruding eyes as indifferent as the eyes of a toad.

His gaze was disconcerting, and I ventured the announcement again, only to see that he was looking beyond me into the fringe of the woods and apparently did not care what I said. I watched him a minute or two, then looked to see what interested him. It was at approximately this spot that I had seen what I thought was the strange apparition called the Abbess only minutes before.

I said now with an embarrassed laugh, "Your famed ghost was standing there a short time ago. Or so I thought."

"Ay," said the coachman, a sound very like a grunt. "It'll be the Abbess ye seen, right enough. Postilion took flight these three days since account of her."

His easy assumption that ghosts stood about eerily frightening coachman's helpers made my own fears seem absurd. Trying to be cheerful, I reminded him, "I feel sure there is nothing dangerous in those woods. I have been standing here opposite for some little time, and no harm has come to me."

At the look he gave me out of those toadlike eyes, I started back, adding defensively, "I daresay your postilion had a powerful imagination."

"Well, ye may say so. It was that Herring-female with her tales. Mark me! And good riddance to the wicked creature."

"Is it the other housekeeper you are speaking of?" I asked, genuinely curious now. This matter was a great deal more important than some sly pseudo-ghost.

"That one, aye. The Herring-rath female. More like to a sneaking spy than to a lady what keeps a great household . . . But we're to fetch up a postilion this night in the village."

So that was what he waited for. Meanwhile, staring very hard at the undergrowth where the coach lights cast each remaining blade of grass into a long black shadow, sharp as a dagger, I could see any number of tree trunks and here and there piled twigs and branches, any of which might have snapped and broken some minutes earlier. I no longer believed that my imagination was so powerful that I had twice within an hour seen an apparition. No doubt, there was a logical explanation. For some reason as yet unknown, I had been followed through the Dalreagh Forest to this place. I did not doubt my pursuer was human. The puzzle to me, as I considered the mystery, was why.

The coachman had turned now and was looking toward the village in the opposite direction. I did likewise, moving over the worn but splendid velvet to the other coach window. I could not get the window open. It was firmly stuck, but through it I saw a tall man striding over the stone bridge from the village. He looked rather mature to be a postilion, and when he came closer, it seemed to my critical eyes that his greatcoat, hat, and boots were all of excellent quality. However, he may have fallen on bad times and taken this post in desperation. I wondered if he could be drunk, for he seemed headed straight toward the coach door; but the coachman said something to him, and he leaped up on the box beside the coachman with an ease surprising in a man who, as I supposed, must have been drinking rum or gin all evening in the local village.

The coachman gave his team the signal to start, and we were on our way around that first tight bend in the estate road. I found I had to clutch the window for my life or, at the very least, to prevent myself from joggling around like a pea in an ill-fitting pod. The thick, wooded dark of the Dalreagh Forest soon thinned out, however, presenting wide, elegant vistas of what must be stunning reaches of lawn during the season and which, even now, under its winter cloak, showed a certain elegance in its dead straw color where, underneath, there was a distinct and glassy shine. The entire region thereabouts was still awash with the recent rains, and it was this water that glistened just under the surface throughout the rolling fields in the area.

The coach and horses rolled and thundered on over the muddy road that now neatly bisected the fields in order to reach the little wooden bridge that led up to the front of a large and curious building, part manor house and part medieval fortress, or so it seemed at this distance. The swollen little river with its high banks, whose meandering our road followed, now flowed past the front of the ancient stone house, where it had been tamed so that it split and ran also in a deep channel along the east side of the house and presumably across the back as well, since I could just see the glimmer of the waters there under the moonlight.

Most of the lower half of the great stone building was in shadows because much of it seemed to be designed for an enclosed walkway, with vaulted roofs shrouded in darkness. Very like the cloisters of a church, I thought, as we approached the little wooden bridge, and this resemblance to a religious edifice was particularly noticeable at the east corner, where the high, cruciform window and vaulted roof emphasized that this might well be the home of Mist House's favorite apparition, the Black Abbess.

It was an extraordinary building, so definitely split in personality. There was the modernized Tudor front on the south and westerly half, with charming mullioned windows and a view of rolling lawns that ended at some little walking distance where the mauve-colored hills put out feelers of limestone in the direction of Mist House. In spring and summer weather, I thought, this must be a bright, green, exquisite haven. But, of course, it was not spring now. However, it was all beautifully illuminated by the high moon and the windy clarity of the night. The abbey corner in the southeast, which was nearest to the bridge approach, faced the river-moat on two sides and, perhaps because of its solemn, medieval aspect, seemed far less attractive or pleasant.

The coach rattled wildly and noisily over the bridge, which felt, judging from my battered form, ready to collapse at any moment. Having crossed this last obstacle, we swung around, pausing briefly before the imitation cloisters that were apparently the entrance to Mist House. This was eastward toward the Abbey portion of the great stone building and much more shadowed than the delightful Tudor section to the west and in the moonlight.

I expected the tall, surprisingly well-dressed postilion to get down and open the carriage door for me, letting down the steps and doing the honors as his first official task in the employment of Mist House. I was a good deal surprised, then, when the two men merely leaped down, the mysterious new postilion easily, the stout coachman with an effort, while the team shifted about, their hooves clattering rhythmically on the grass-grown cobblestones as if to remind me that I must move quickly. As I put my hand to the door, assuming this was to be a household where the housekeeper counted very low in the scale of service, I saw the postilion make a quick, impatient gesture, and to my surprise, the coachman obeyed him on the instant. I was ushered out and down the steps by a deeply bowing coachman and found myself directly beneath the series of archs that formed the imitation cloister.

I saw now that the cloister appeared to join the comfortable Tudor portion to the west with the severe and awe-inspiring corner of the medieval abbey on the east. It was too late in the evening, however, for me to pay great attention to the facades of my position. What concerned me a great deal more was the reaction of those within the household, whose impression of me would make my task easy or difficult. I confess, also, that I more than half expected Lucie Dalreagh herself to be on hand so that I should at least feel my presence was awaited. Whether I proved successful or not depended, in great part, on the confidence my employers placed in me.

The new postilion had gone to the heads of the two lead horses and soothed first one, then the other, in a way that I could not but admire for its success with the capricious and curiously frightened animals.

"What are they afraid of?" I called to the postilion while the coachman brought my portmanteau up and with his free hand opened a door for me halfway along the covered walk.

"These beauties?" said the postilion, slapping the flank of one long, dark creature, who seemed to understand that the gesture was a loving one. "They are like the others who inhabit the enchanted woods. They have acquired an imagination."

This told me very little except that whatever had startled the teams, the coachman, and me tonight, it was probably, as I had expected, quite human and that the new servant possessed a good deal of common sense, a surprising quality in my experience with lesser servants.

I stepped into a small stone room so cold and so ancient I knew it must belong to the abbey part of the house. There were dusty weapons hanging on the walls, a solitary trestle table, and long benches about the room. Long ago, this unfriendly place must have been the guard room and later, no doubt, served as the porter's office. A door across the room opposite the entrance seemed to open of itself, and I started, then pretended not to have revealed this insecurity which would look so badly to my new employers.

A sallow young woman with dark eyes, a fine Roman nose, and a sullen mouth stood behind the door. Something proud in her stance and her expression told me she was not the parlormaid that her plain, unfashionable garments suggested. As a matter of fact, I rather suspect no parlormaid would dress so meanly. I did not know how to address her. Nothing about her or the house presented a friendly greeting to me; but it was not, nor ever had been, the business of a housekeeper to be received like a guest.

"Good evening," I said as pleasantly as I could amid this freezing climate, both physical and emotional. "I am Anne Killain, employed by Mrs. Dalreagh as housekeeper . . ." And as she stood there barring my way, I went on, with a slight edge to my voice, "Will you be so good as to summon Mrs. Dalreagh?"

She shrugged and glanced behind me at the coachman, who set my portmanteau on the cold, uncarpeted stone floor.

"You may go, Cedric."

The coachman obeyed her so promptly that I knew she must be a member of the family, and obviously the only personage she fitted was Amanda Dalreagh. At once, I could understand the antagonism between her and her stepmother; for if she was the daughter of the house, no two women could be less alike than Amanda Dalreagh and that poor, weak soul, Lucie Fairburn.

"Miss Dalreagh?" I asked, curtsying respectfully. "I am sorry to have arrived at this unseasonable hour, but the Accommodation Coach nearly overturned."

For an instant, I thought the girl would send me packing, but she looked me over scornfully from head to foot. I could not mistake her dislike, and she said abruptly, "As I thought. She would invite a creature with all the obvious attractions to defend her. She cannot even protect her insipid self."

I had picked up my portmanteau, but I hesitated before moving forward.

"Your pardon, ma'am. I am persuaded you do not wish me to understand you. Will you ring for a servant to show me to my quarters, or shall I?"

The girl—for in spite of her scornful dignity, she was scarcely over sixteen—said coldly, "I daresay you will not fear to share the previous housekeeper's bed with her shadow."

Looking around the room in which we stood, I smiled, a cool, professional smile that served to remind us of our places: the powerless relation to the mistress of the house and the chief servant of the household staff, who has her own authority and, if she is wise, wields that authority quietly, but firmly. The room was at the end of an el-shaped great hall that must have been centuries old. It had enormous vaulted ceilings hung with banners whose coating of dust did no credit to the housekeeprs of the past at Mist House. This end of the hall was evidently used as a kind of formal parlor or lounge; for a number of items of comfortable furniture, couches, taborets, and lamps had been set about, looking absurd against the enormous stone walls to the east, which, I suspected, led to the section of the house that was a part of the old abbey.

I said politely, "Mrs. Herrenrath's shadow will be much too busy following her to her next post. A good housekeeper needs many helping hands. Don't you agree, Miss Dalreagh?"

For some unaccountable reason, this seemed to throw her into a dreadful passion. Her black eyes snapped, and her jaw, like her nose, a heavy appurtenance to her face, set in an unbecoming line.

"You may be as flippant as you like, but mark me, you'll play no spy upon me and mine. And don't imagine you will. You think I do not know what happened to my poor Papa in that dreadful creature's hands? When I get the money for their hire, the Bow Street Runners will track down the truth. And it will not be the first murder they have come upon!"

I was so shocked I scarcely knew how to answer her wild ravings.

"Believe me, Miss Dalreagh, I had no notion I should be so unwelcome at Mist House nor that there was any question of . . . of a crime having been committed. In such case, I shall be the first to ask that an investigation be made and to oblige the persons in any way that my employers see fit. But . . . are you sure of your facts? I was led to believe—"

"Amanda!" said a pleasant but authoritative male voice behind me, "Will you ring for a servant and allow Miss Killain to proceed on her way? It is growing late, and she will be in want of rest."

I turned around, finding this silent observer behind me even more disturbing than the ugly dislike of the daughter of the house. I thought I recognized the tone of that male voice, and when I saw the "postilion" in a clear light, I realized that my first impression had been correct. He was much too elegantly dressed to be a stable servant and looked rather more like my late husband's class of aristocrat. Though he was a man taller than the average and undeniably attractive, his manner, his cool blue eyes, and the way he held his head, with its windblown, russet-colored hair, suggested that he could be more cutting and give one a more severe setdown than anything the girl, Amanda, might contrive. She flushed at his presence, or his interference, then cried out one last objection to me.

"But she is that creature's paid spy, Uncle. Don't you see?"

At the word "uncle," I stared at the gentleman, a little shaken when I considered my early assumption that one of the first peers of Britain, the Earl of Dalreagh, was a coachman's helper. Although embarrassed, I found the notion funny, and when I caught his eye, I realized he too must be remembering this, for it was quite astounding how personable the haughty gentleman looked when he smiled, as now.

"Yes. I am Dalreagh, as I suppose you are wondering, Miss Killain. I could not contrive the simple hire of a postilion. They refuse me with the most cowardly candor. I trust you will manage the business with dispatch."

I had sunk to a respectful curtsy, but he gave me his hand in a charming way which went far to destroy the unpleasantness of my first few minutes in Mist House. I did not look at his niece, whom I now conceived to be hardened in her aversion to me after the Earl's interference, and I did not want her to believe I took pleasure in thwarting her.

"I hope I shall carry out all orders to the

satisfaction of those who issue them, my Lord," I said quietly and was about to ask which member of the family would give me my daily instructions, but I thought it wiser to wait until we were away from Miss Amanda.

"Amanda, *will* you oblige me by ringing?" he reminded his niece with a return of that pleasant but unmistakable air of command which the girl could not ignore.

"If you wish, Uncle." She went around the corner of the el-shaped Great Hall and reached for a musty velvet bellpull under the eye of the Earl. Seeing that she was obeying, he turned his attention to me.

I had the uneasy notion that he was assessing my qualifications, both physical and mental, piece by piece and part by part, which would not have been so disturbing in a man less personally endowed. Miss Amanda had already tugged on the velvet bellpull when he said suddenly, "It's of no consequence. I will take Miss Killain to the quarters assigned to her." I do not know which of us, the girl or I, was the more surprised when he picked up my portmanteau. Then he asked, "What quarters are they, by the by?"

Miss Amanda paused a fraction of time, long enough for me to guess she was assigning me some place not occupied by the previous housekeepers and, I was reasonably sure, not likely to be very pleasant.

"I . . . I believe they are in the passage of the Abbey Wing. The second door on the right, once you have passed the gallery."

The Earl took my arm lightly, but I suspected, even from this touch, that he was a man of considerable strength. His height, the long greatcoat he wore, and his cool-eyed gaze gave him an illusion of slim arrogance. I was soon to discover the illusion was in some ways a reality, but the physical strength had been rather a surprise. He was not the sort of man who would need to depend on muscular prowess to win his way.

We were on our way across the lengthy Great Hall, whose roof, with many time-darkened beams, was as high as the modern portion of Mist House. Being at that moment extraordinarily sensitive to the slightest nuance, the most subtle stirring of air around me, I thought, "I am being watched." It was an absurd thought after my similar suspicions in the forest earlier, and I did not suppose there was anything of the phantom about this person, but it did annoy me not to know where the person was standing and who it was, and that old and bothersome question—why?—arose again.

Undoubtedly, it was Amanda Dalreagh. I looked back, but she had already closed the door and was gone.

I glanced up at my surroundings, pretending

a mere housekeeper's interest, but the feeling would not leave. How tiresome for some silly, curious person to be this way, I thought. How tiresome—and how eery.

3

His Lordship, Richard Dalreagh, was striding toward a flight of stone steps that mounted as they turned in semicircular fashion until they disappeared behind a high stone column. No other human being was in the Great Hall or on the steps in front of us, so far as I could see, but as my gaze traveled upward, I saw that there were windowlike apertures high along the inner wall, and I guessed that a gallery must run along behind those apertures on what would be the equivalent of more than two stories above the ground floor. It would be easy enough for some person to watch us crossing the Great Hall toward the steps without himself being seen. I shivered at the thought, and the Earl glanced at me.

"Do you feel the chill? These old houses are full of drafty corners, I'm afraid."

I appreciated this little apology, which was not a common thing in my experience and showed his good breeding and concern for others, I thought.

"No, my Lord. It was only a . . . sensation. I

thought someone was watching us. Lucie—Mrs. Dalreagh, perhaps."

"Not Lucie," he said so abruptly that I stared at him. "A servant, probably. We are a lonely people here and rather isolated. The last estate before the hills. The servants are naturally interested in every new inmate, since they are all shut in here for weeks at a time when the weather is stormy. That is undoubtedly how the tales get out. The previous housekeeper was an adept at it. We had to get rid of her."

The cool, dispassionate way in which he mentioned getting rid of Mrs. Herrenrath did not relieve my chills.

"Then, I will not see Mrs. Dalreagh tonight?" I asked, trying to use the same indifferent tones. The truth is, I was remembering once when I went to a great house in this fashion, only to be told that the young lady who had summoned me was dead. Apparently, no such shock was liable to occur now, for His Lordship said, "Tomorrow will be soon enough, I should imagine. She has a problem, as you may be aware. She is a somnambulist and considerable rest is recommended."

"Yes. I know. I saw her walking the other night at the school."

"Good. The unfortunate young woman got scant sympathy from my niece or from the woman who formerly had your post. It is my belief that a measure of calm and freedom from this fretting about ghosts and apparitions will go far toward curing her." He looked at me curiously. "I should not have thought you were friends. The girl is not your sort at all. A hopeless ninny."

I did not know what to reply to that frankness and was relieved to devote my attention to something else.

We were close to the top of the steps now, and I saw that the top step fanned out upon a long gallery which, as I had suspected, contained many windows. On the left were the glassed windows opening on the inner courtyard three stories below, and on the right were the openings in stone about the level of my own eyes by which a person could see all that went on in the Great Hall below without himself being seen. At the same time Lord Dalreagh startled me by the rather contemptuous remark, "Ah! I think I can guess our eavesdropper. You see the door at the far end of the gallery?"

I saw more. The door was closing, but not rapidly enough to hide the slender, black-clad form of a man shorter than the Earl, probably about my own height, which is not inconsiderable for a woman.

"Good heavens!" My exclamation was not for the identity of the man but for the idea that he found so little occupation he must tiptoe about, watching from rather large peepholes.

"I assure you," said the Earl in his sardonic voice, "you will find him the epitome of all that is beautiful in the human male, and we shall have you swooning on our hands when he refuses your overtures." He glanced at me, saw that I did not know whether to look shocked or to laugh, and shook my arm a little. "Come now. Please laugh. We really are a beggarly lot of brooding sour faces here, and you need not worry about offending him. He cannot hear us. He is my niece's French tutor, Monsieur Louis Minotte. Quite harmless, I assure you—except, I am given to understand, where the female heart is concerned."

Privately, I thought it difficult for any woman of a strong and passionate nature like myself to find comfort in whatever shallow, watery feelings encompassed the Lucie Dalreaghs of the world. But I wondered at the curious behavior of Monsieur Minotte all the same. How could it possibly interest him to spy on the family and their doings? In any case, I yielded to my own inclination as well as my companion's desire and laughed at his little joke. I confess that in this first hour of our acquaintance, it gave me pleasure to oblige him.

I found the dimly lit Long Gallery a strange place, with its windows and peepholes, the sensation it gave one of walking on a rooftop or on a ceiling. No matter which way I looked, to my left down upon the chill inner courtyard now shrouded in the most intense darkness or to my right, where I glanced through one of the peepholes upon the beams and the Great Hall far below, I always had the sensation of peering downward. I said as much to the Earl.

"And there is higher still to this ancient pile, Miss Killain," he told me. "A section which Lucie or my niece will very likely show you tomorrow. We have a fine assortment of battlements with crenellations and all the other appurtenances to romance, though, I regret to say, we disappointed Lucie when she first observed our rooftops."

"How so?"

"We could provide her with no fair maiden who plunged off the battlements to her death to escape the lascivious attentions of a Dalreagh."

This time I laughed very frankly. "What a pity you should be so disobliging! But no. Quite the contrary. I believe the complaint hereabouts is that a Black Abbess yielded too quickly to the attentions of a Dalreagh."

"Yes," he agreed sadly. "I fear some people—and some ghosts—are never satisfied."

When we both smiled at this thought, I found myself deeply aware of the gentleman's own not inconsiderable charm. He might jestingly boast the romantic qualities of his niece's

French tutor, but I took leave to doubt that Monsieur Minotte would arouse in me that same sense of warmth, excitement, and deference which made me just a trifle shy in His Lordship's presence. I found that the company of Richard Dalreagh took my mind very neatly off the chilling cold in the Long Gallery.

"I understand the windows that look on the courtyard," I said. "But why are there so many peepholes above the Great Hall?"

"Chronic mistrust, I fear, or a born curiosity to see what one's dinner guests were up to. This section of the building is still a part of the Abbey that was a power in the North two hundred years before the Conquest. It is a thousand years old and looks it, I'm sure. Small wonder that phantoms are seen floating about here and there. Monsieur Minotte has interested Lucie in them. He intends to write a dictionary of apparitions, I believe, in somewhat the same style as Dr. Johnson provided for his lexicon. But even less lively, I expect, for our Frenchman is a gentleman not much given to humor."

It was very dark as we stepped down several stairs into the stone passage to which Amanda Dalreagh had directed us, and as we passed a branch of candles at the top of the stairs before leaving the Gallery, the Earl took it up and held it high for us to descend. He looked around, frowning.

"This cannot be right. The passage hasn't been dusted in weeks. What in heaven's name is the girl about to send you here?"

I suspected what Miss Amanda was about but said nothing. It was not my place to criticize my quarters but, rather, to make them and the rest of the house presentable, as well as to organize the servants efficiently. He tried the latch on the second door, and I knew at once that no member of the servant household had been at work on this ancient chamber for months, perhaps years.

"What the devil is that girl thinking of?" Dalreagh exclaimed in such a chilling voice that I pitied the unfortunate Amanda already. He raised the candle branch, nearly setting afire the huge and dusty cobweb that hung from a bedpost to the big, ironbound chest below the foot of the bed. A small squeaking sound somewhere on the floor made me laugh, a sound that startled my companion.

"It is only a mouse under the bed," I said, seeing that he was stalking about, prepared for bigger prey.

"It is no laughing matter, and that I assure you!"

But the sight of this musty old haven of spiders and other creatures of the dark and then the cloud of mold and dust that spread over us like a miasma when he struck the bed coverings with his fist were too much for us both, and half coughing and half laughing at the absurdity of anyone sleeping there that night, we backed off toward the open door.

"It could be a charming room," I remarked, contradicting his flat statement that nothing could be more hideous, "with a good airing, windows and floors and walls cleaned, fresh linen. The room must be exceedingly old, perhaps belonging to the abbot himself before the Norman Conquest. Only think of—"

"I am thinking! The Abbey crypt is no worse than this. Good God! I had no notion things had come to such a pass."

My voice wavered slightly as I wavered within.

"You . . . you have a crypt? Here? In the building?"

"Beneath the old chapel. That's on the front of the building, you will remember. The Great Hall has a door opening into the chapel. Yes. The sisters were buried on the premises. You enter the crypt from a flight of steps in one corner of the chapel." Seeing my obvious dislike of the idea that we slept above dead nuns and abbesses, his eyes lighted in a way which suggested he was amused at my expression. "All exceedingly good women, I'm sure, Miss Killain. They should not be likely to haunt you, unless, of course, you are sleeping in one of the beds they inhabited in life. You must allow them to haunt you then. Any self-respecting abbess would do so."

"It is a very odd abbess, indeed, who sleeps in a bed of this grandeur," I said wryly, gesturing toward the worn hangings and the once-splendid coverlet.

He took my arm and ushered me out into the passage, and presently, we came to a sharp right-angle turn, and I found myself in a much more modern sector of the building. I guess by his silence that he had been considering various possibilities, and now he turned to me abruptly in front of an imposing door.

"My brother's—" he bit his lip and amended, "my late brother's bedchamber was here, and for sentimental reasons, it has been kept much as it was before his death. With the exception of the apartments belonging to members of the family and to Minotte, this is the only one I know, of a certainty, that you will find clean and comfortable. Do you object to spending the night in the room in which Kevin died?"

"Not at all, my Lord," I lied with what I considered exemplary calm. "You are very good."

Having pushed the door open, he took my arm. "And you are very—" Our eyes met momentarily in one of those tiny pauses, so pregnant with thoughts, between two persons. His cool, polite manner broke the awkward pause.

"Very capable, I am sure. But come in. Come in. See what you think of it."

What could I think of it but that it was absurdly elegant for an upper servant? And it was a splendid room in every feature, the elegance of the furniture, masculine, of course, but not oppressively so, and everything in the forefront of good taste, besides being of the period, only a few years back, that we now look on as a clean delight in Grecian lines. The bed hangings were simple: no curtains, only the canopy overhead. There was a large Jacobean clothespress, but otherwise nothing overwhelming, and the crisp cleanliness of sheets, the soft cleanliness of carpet and cushions, all joined to entice me, for I was very tired and just a trifle depressed. I did not know why. All houses, perhaps, seem strange and unfriendly on the first entrance of the hireling.

"Can you be comfortable tonight?" the Earl asked in his warm and sympathetic tone, which surprised me again in such a self-sufficient man.

"Quite comfortable, thank you. Your Lordship is a great deal too kind." As I curtsied, he took my hand as before and raised me up.

"Don't be excessively modest, Miss Killain. You deserve well of us. I only hope we do not frighten you away . . . I will send up a maid with warm water and towels. And then, I trust you will have an uninterrupted sleep. No night visitants." He smiled at my expression and left me.

I remained in the doorway, watching him until he disappeared around the angle in the passage, and then I wondered why he chose to return that long, dark, chilly way through the old Abbey remains rather than through the modern westerly half of the building, which was inevitably quicker and cleaner. Perhaps, he was curious to see how many other dusty, disused chambers there were along that sinister and somehow rather sad old passage. No matter. If I was permitted to retain my post here, I would rescue the poor sad rooms from their present inhabitants.

Shortly after, there was a faint scratching on the panel of the door, and when I called to come in, a tow-headed, bosomy young woman, looking sulky at having been summoned at this hour, appeared with hot water and exquisitely fringed napkins. I felt so contaminated by the dust and dirt of those passages and their offshoots that I shot the bolt on the door and set about washing from head to foot.

I was so busy that I did not have time to think about the last inhabitant of this chamber until I was dressing for bed and searched for the steps or footstool with which to mount the bed. There was none, which reminded me of the man who had not needed a stool by which to mount the bed . . . the bed on which he had died so very oddly, to judge from his daughter's troubling words.

After a brief struggle with my imagination, which persisted in flashing before my eyes an entire deathbed scene, I clambered up into bed and closed my eyes, thinking I had never been so tired. With the perversity of fate, my eyes at once opened wide, as I remembered that I hadn't the least idea where I should report in the morning or to whom. I was not even sure that I could find my own way down to the kitchens. However, there was an elegant plum-colored plush bellpull just beyond the bed, and I supposed I could always summon a maid or footman to lead me in the correct way.

It must have been some time after midnight. My little watch, the only jewelry with which I escaped from Royalist France, had stopped, and I could only guess at the hour; but the wind was dying, and the cold moon had swung far across the starry heavens. I felt of the bedclothes, marvelling at their softness, which came of good material often laundered, and then I wondered again about the last person who had slept in this great, comfortable bed. *And died in this bed.*

I tried to recall what Miss Hunnicut and Lucie had told me about the man's death and how their words could possibly fit the horrid picture his daughter had drawn when she talked of my spying on the household in her stepmother's behalf and of murder, and then her accusation against poor, simple Lucie. Was it possible that the Honorable Kevin Dalreagh actually had been murdered? Certainly, the knowing Lancashire woman on the coach had mentioned poison. It might be one of those gossipy items that contains much more imagination than truth, but the small kernel of truth that may have started the gossip was the thing I would like to have tracked down.

However, all was probably explained by the abrupt dismissal of Mrs. Herrenrath from this household. She would very likely have been responsible for any ill her clacking tongue could do to the Dalreaghs. For a brief few seconds, I wondered why she had not yet reported to Mrs. Shane-Porter in London in search of another post. But I really was very tired. The rough coach ride and the walk afterward had been more wearing than a full day's work as scullery maid, which was how I started in domestic service under dear Miss Hunnicut, and without even snuffing the candle left by the Earl, I went off to sleep.

Toward morning, the candle had burned down to its socket, and I was awakened by the careful moving of the latch on the door. I sat straight up in bed, still half asleep, and wondering in an idiotic state of suspense if that could be Kevin Dalreagh returning to occupy his property. Whoever was trying the latch seemed most furtive, so I knew it could not be a regular morning visit of the usual sort. A maid with my morning tea tray would certainly knock or set the tray outside the door.

"Who is it?" I asked in a voice—the faintness of which annoyed me so much that I went on with more authority, "What do you wish?"

I thought I heard some sort of dim reply outside, swallowed by the vastness of the Mist House corridors, and I reached for my robe, then slid down off the high bed, and not being able to locate my night slippers, I went across the room barefoot and shivering, for I had carelessly let the little fire in the grate die down like the candle.

I opened the door, letting in a great blast of arctic air from the passage and almost missed the little man who stood there, patient and still, until I finally saw him. The top of his white head reached my chin, and his little blue eyes had a sweet, friendly expression whose influence it was impossible to avoid.

"I am most excessively happy to see you, miss," he assured me, raising his bed candle the better to examine me. "I had supposed this room was inhabited by my late son-in-law, which, I confess, would make me somewhat uneasy."

I agreed silently that ghosts of the dead, especially the murdered dead, made me more than a trifle uneasy, but he said, gazing at me in his ingenuous way, like an aged infant, " 'Pon my word, but you are pretty . . . I am Amanda's grandpapa. My poor daughter was married to Kevin, you know. That is to say, you do belong in this house by daylight, do you not? I should feel ever so foolish to discover I had been conversing with a phantom. Not," he added politely, "that it would not be a very interesting experience."

I bobbed a small curtsy in my night robes, assuring him that I was very much alive and was the new housekeeper. I asked him if I could serve him in some way. He was breathing in tight, quick little gasps, as if after strong exertion, or perhaps because he was an asthmatic.

"Oh no. Not in the least, at the moment. If you are to take over Old Herring's domain, then I will have a small bill of particulars drawn up to present to you tomorrow morning. That is to say," he peered into my room and beyond between the half-closed portieres at the sky, "this morning. I am persuaded, my dear, that you will oblige me in the little attentions to my needs which an old man requires."

I stood on my half-frozen left foot, thawing the other against my left ankle.

"Certainly, sir. As soon as it is light. You—er—you did not wish those things to be done on the instant, I suppose."

"No, indeed. I should not dream of troubling you." Nevertheless, he breathed so heavily and with such effort that I pushed the door open wide, saying with alarm, "Do sit down a moment, sir. You are unwell."

He was wheezing badly when I helped him in, and his hands shook so that I removed his candlestick and held it. But once he was seated in a great milord chair by the door and looking smaller, more shriveled than ever, he became calm, and having his hands free, he put one into the pocket of his long, heavy overrobe. Either he had not got to bed yet or he had dressed in order to come and visit the ghostly son-in-law he expected to find in this room.

But that did not concern me for long. He pulled out of his pocket a really horrible little weapon, a knife which might have originally sharpened quill pens but looked dangerously lethal to me.

"Is . . . is that yours, sir?" I asked, hoping against hope that he would tell me he had merely found it.

"Oh yes. It is mine. And ever so sharp. Cuts into the flesh as if it were eggshell."

I wondered just how he knew.

4

"How did you happen to come here at this hour, sir?"

The little man turned over that ugly, shimmering weapon in a puzzled way. He glanced up at me, perplexed.

"It was foolish, was it not? I could hardly use this against a ghostly son-in-law. I am Sir Peveril Wye, my dear. But in any case, I saw the light through that window and I came all the way up to see if I could catch . . ."

His voice drifted off into vague shrugs and a look at me that plainly called for help.

"Yes, sir? You desired to catch someone. But how could you have seen my light?"

He started to rise but was so unsteady I took pity on him and nodded as though I perfectly understood when he waved at some distant place to the left of the window.

"My room is there. Floor beneath, on the corner. But I can see this room. And often in the night, I see a shadow . . ."

"You must be very tired," I said, feeling deeply sorry for the vague little man. "Shall I walk with you to your room?"

He stared at me, much struck by my mental agility at reading his true desires.

"Do you know, my dear, I believe you are right. That is exactly what I would like above anything. Come along. I will play the gallant, as I did in my youth. I was rather popular among the ladies, you know."

"I am quite sure you were. Would you oblige me by carrying the bed candle? Then I will carry—" I reached for the knife and very nearly had it in my grasp when he recovered hastily.

"No, no, my dear. Sharp instruments must always be kept from young ladies. They are most unladylike."

I could not deny this, nor could I point out that in my experience, housekeepers were not considered ladies. He retained the knife while I walked beside him, carefully guiding his footsteps. It was absurdly done, and I do not know what I was thinking about that I did not take a candle of my own; for once the little man was safe in his quaint but oddly charming corner room again, I was left to make my own way back along the corridor on this floor of the modern Mist House and then up carpeted stairs to my own passage, which joined the new and the old sections of the building. It was considerable walking in the dark and required me to behave rather like a theatrical Lady Macbeth, with my arm stretched out before me, to feel the way.

Since it was shortly before dawn, I was able to glimpse very vaguely the contours of walls and objects in my path. I reached the staircase and began to mount the steps which started in a westerly direction, then turned sharply and mounted northward toward the passage which had been assigned to me. Quite suddenly, I heard the clatter of those ancient iron-shod clogs often worn by villagers of the North counties, and I slowed my step in order to avoid a close meeting there in the dark.

I was too late, however. The clatter of clogs came nearer, and suddenly, just as I stepped up on the landing at the turn of the steps, we confronted each other, the ladies' maid in her neat uniform, I in my flowing robes, my hair hanging loose down my back, my face undoubtedly a pale glimmer in this half-dark, lighted only by an uncurtained window at the end of the upper passage.

There was a sudden shriek, so loud, so ear-splitting that I nearly stumbled back down the steps. Fortunately, I was somewhat prepared, and when the girl opened her mouth again, having scarcely glanced at me, I guessed what was to come. I put my hand out.

"No, no! The Abbess! Don't touch me!" she shrieked.

I shook her as gently as I could. The outcome

was that she recovered in a time slightly less than she might have.

"Calm yourself!" I said sternly. "I am Miss Killain, the new housekeeper. Hired to replace Mrs. Herrenrath. You understand?"

It was an effort, but she pulled herself together. I sympathized, yet could scarcely do more than ask, "What are you doing in the corridor at this hour?"

She fumbled, seeming as afraid of the real flesh and blood me as she was of the phantom she had conjured up. She managed to bob a curtsy, saying, "I was sent to fetch hot shaving water for His Lordship, the Earl. I did not know there was anyone up at this hour."

I felt ashamed for having startled her.

"I understand. Forgive me. I did not intend to frighten you. Go on about your errand, and—" It was no use. She was hardly listening. She was still shaking.

"I did not mean to scream so, madam. But I was so frightened I nearly jumped out of my skin."

She made an effort at another curtsy, but I had to help her up, and she hurried on. I stood aside, knowing from past experience what it is to encounter a new superior, and at an odd moment like this. It is quite true that in my case at Mist House, my employer might be a person as gentle and unassuming as Lucie Dalreagh, but the paymistress was generally the housekeeper, the woman who watched the behavior of the servants with a basilisk eye. I nearly always got on well with the persons under me, but occasionally, I was feared, and I understood this feeling only too well. I had not learned my own lessons in an easy school.

It was dawn by the time I reached my room and looked out of the window on a world that seemed as washed and clean and golden as Eden must have been. I stood by the window, studying the scene and wondering how it happened that I had supposed the place to be so evil. It was strange, of course, and there were two or three rather unconventional episodes, such as Monsieur Minotte watching us from the peephole in the Long Gallery and then that odd little man whose daughter had been Kevin Dalreagh's first wife. But these could scarcely be called evils.

I turned, went back to the dead man's great bed, and climbed up with some slight exertion, hoping I would not be disturbed until I had had a few more hours' rest. I do not recall whether my sleep was of very long duration, but I remember vividly that I was aroused by a disturbance outside the door of Kevin Dalreagh's chamber. This time, there could be no question but that the interference was purely physical.

I heard a high-pitched female voice which sounded very like the poor girl I had nearly frightened to death on the staircase in the night.

"But she is, miss. In this very chamber. I seen 'er meself. She come in the night. And no' but a single bag. Portmanteau, they do call 'em."

"I know. I know," an abrupt young female voice cut in. "But how dare she come into Papa's very chamber? I could kill her! Sly, spying beast that she is."

I knew, then, with a horrid sinking feeling, that the voice belonged to Amanda Dalreagh. I got out of bed, seized my overrobe, and went to the door. The latch and the bolt stuck, probably because I closed them hastily and impatiently, but the grating sound warned the women in the corridor, and when I came out, the nervous maid was scuttling away down the corridor. I stood face to face with Miss Amanda, who scowled in the way that was beginning to seem her normal expression. It was, of course, most unbecoming to her features, which were heavy and somber at best, but what concerned me was the absolute hatred she seemed to feel for me. I knew it must be but the residue of that feeling she had against Lucie, her stepmother, and this was far more difficult to combat than a simple prejudice against a new and untried housekeeper.

Trying to placate her, I said, "I shall remove from here at once, miss. But His Lordship could find no other bedchamber prepared at such a late hour."

She had the grace to look very self-conscious at my words, and of course, her attitude reminded me that she was partly responsible, having sent me to that ancient, cobwebbed room in the Abbey section.

"Yes. I fear you were wrongly directed." She seemed almost as if she would apologize but suddenly asked me in the young, ingenuous way that became her very much, "Was Uncle very cross?"

"Only for a moment. I'll have all those old chambers aired and cleaned." I smiled. "Then, you can send all the housekeepers there with the perfect ease of conscience."

She nodded, looked into the chamber over my shoulder, and glanced around.

"I'm sorry. I did not wish to be so rude. You have not disturbed Papa's chamber . . . very much. Do you . . . would you like me to show you to the staff dining room? Were you served tea this morning?"

I explained that none of the servants had known I was in this chamber, and I would appreciate her kindness in showing me down to the staff dining room. She looked after the disappearing servant girl, who seemed to have slowed her steps in the obvious effort to eavesdrop.

Amanda stepped into her father's room to

stand by the window, looking out over the landscape while I dressed quickly.

"It is a lovely day, is it not?" I asked, seeing the vivid blue winter sky and the big patch of sunlight on the carpet.

"We've been having splendid open weather, except for yesterday's early rain. Did you sleep well last night?"

I glanced at her, but the question seemed innocent enough.

"I was visited once. Rather an odd meeting."

Amanda's fingers tightened their grip on the portieres. She kept her face averted.

"Really? Then you saw—something?"

"Some *one,* I should say. Your grandfather came up to this room. He said he had seen the candlelight."

"Oh. Grandpapa ... I wonder what he knows."

I paused in the act of brushing my hair. I watched her face reflected in Kevin Dalreagh's shaving mirror. She seemed extraordinarily ill at ease and thoughtful.

"I don't believe I understand you, miss. What should Sir Peveril know?"

"How Papa died, of course."

I suppressed a start and finished my toilette. There was nothing I could say to that curious and unsettling remark. Apparently, Miss Amanda was not the only member of the household who suspected that Kevin Dalreagh's death was murder. I could not imagine why they felt that he had not died of a disease, as was generally supposed. And what grounds would there be for anyone to murder him?

I said this aloud as I joined her at the window which faced out on the back of the building. She did not look at me but went on staring outward at the scene that was well worth our attention. On the near horizon lay the sharp, dark hills, mauve-colored in the morning light. Between those not too distant hills and the diverted water that formed a moat around Mist House, the rolling, partially wooded ground was divided by frequently placed low stone walls.

Avoiding my question, she murmured, "Sometimes, I think our lives, mine in any case, are like those hills. Everything looks so fair, but as long as I've lived, I've always noticed those dreadful black clouds that you can see now concealing the peak tops. They do glower at one."

I understood, in part, how a life spent in one situation, forever under the faint shadow of those peaks, might give Miss Amanda her grim notions, but I said briskly, hoping to cheer her, "We must remember, miss, that there are times when the clouds are white and the air is pure. And perhaps that is also true of our lives, don't you think so?"

Disdain crossed her face once more.

"And well you may say. A woman like you is sure to find it easy to take a new post. But for others, life is hard, let me tell you." As I looked at her, puzzled at this absurd misunderstanding of a servant's life, she added the explanation that enlightened me. "I have seen it happen before. Like Papa, who chose beauty over sense." I could only assume that she referred to her stepmother, Lucie Dalreagh. "And what is more absurd, others have done the same."

I wondered if the "others" might be her Uncle Richard. I rather hoped not. He did not appear to be so easily deluded by appearances.

"Are you ready, Miss Killain? Come along," she said in a sharp voice far too old for her years.

"Certainly. I am ready." And we walked out and along the hall into the older Abbey section of the building. I had thought there might be a shorter way, through the new wing, past the fine, elegant closed doors I had seen the night before after escorting little Sir Peveril Wye to his room, but instead, I recognized the ancient passage, the doors of spider-haunted rooms to which Amanda had sent His Lordship and me. I soon saw the high, vaulted ceiling of the Long Gallery, and as we passed, I glanced for the first time through the windows toward the sunlit courtyard.

There was a fountain in the center, with

water foaming up to spray the nearest cobblestones. I did not have time to admire the construction of the fountain itself; for I had noticed a woman seated on the rim of the stone bowl, her head bowed. Often, as the water splashed out and downward, it sprinkled her fair hair, leaving little droplets that caught the light. I was sure it was Lucie Dalreagh whom I had seen there in such a dejected position and wondered at her despair. I pitied her profoundly, but, I confess, I could not quite sympathize with such a weak acceptance of fate. Nor could I quite believe that she was so shattered over the death, some weeks gone by, of a man like Kevin Dalreagh, who had mistreated her.

Despite my own feelings, which almost approximated those of Lucie's stepdaughter, or so I thought, I felt an instant resentment when Miss Amanda, seeing the little tableau that had touched me, nudged me away from the window and reminded me, "She is forever unhappy. Or so she seems. It's of no account that she married Papa or that he . . . he died and she is rich. No! That is all gone for nothing."

I said quickly, "Do the doors on the courtyard permit others to watch her? I should think there would be more privacy for grief."

Amanda looked at me, one quick, contemptuous glance.

"Truly? You are concerned for her grief? But yes. I should have remembered. We must not make an unhappy moment for our delicate Madam Dalreagh. You are the spy for her. You will pat her delicate hands, which may have fed the poison—"

"Miss Amanda!" I was truly shocked at her attitude, though I understood well enough the love for her father that lay behind this twisted hatred. "I have no defense for Madam. But for the kitchen's sake and for the good setting of table for all the Dalreagh gentry, I do hope that you will help me to my tasks . . . Any hint of what will better suit the household . . . I shall be vastly obliged if you will give me your good counsel in time."

Miss Amanda acted as though she had not been persuaded by anything I said; yet, I could not but be sensitive to the undercurrents there.

"Miss Killain," she said stiffly, after we had gone on a few steps, "she did not love Papa, don't you understand? She does not love . . . the next who loves her. It is all sham, that pretense of hers. The tears. The rest of it."

Whether this might be true or not, the cynicism of this young girl was genuinely disturbing, but I knew that I should gain nothing by arguing before we quite understood each other. We went on down the steps into the Great Hall, a singularly lonely place, even by daylight. The furnishings, while splendid, the great, dusty banners hanging from the beams, the long trestle tables elegantly refurbished, were still, in their basic simplicity, very much as they had been in ages past. The high roof, whose beams were opposite the Long Gallery, three stories above the ground, gave every sound in the hall a peculiar echo that proved distracting and made me remember how I had seen the tutor, Louis Minotte, watching the Earl and me last night. I looked over my shoulder, a gesture which seemed to amuse Amanda.

"What fustian, Miss Killain! I suppose you fancy the Abbess is in one of those dark corners, her hollow eyes staring at you, marking you for the next to die."

I pretended to find this rather funny.

We went from the Great Hall out through one side of the cloisters that surrounded the now warm and sunny courtyard. We crossed the courtyard toward the north cloister in the rear, where I guessed the servants' quarters and their public rooms would be situated. Lucie Dalreagh was no longer at the fountain. However, she had dropped a bright, lacey square of white muslin, and when I stooped to pick it up, Miss Amanda looked at my hand scornfully.

"A trifling souvenir? You had best save it, madam. It will fetch a handsome price from those who imagine they love her."

A male voice, sharp, harsh, and so agitated that I did not at first note its foreign sound, cut into our slightly sardonic conversation. I was startled by the appearance as much as the voice of the black-clad young man who stood in the doorway at the northwest corner of the garden, behind the cloister.

"If you please, you have the property of Madame Dalreagh. Give it to me!"

I guessed by his French accent that the young gentleman who accosted me in this reckless fashion was Miss Amanda's tutor in French and Courtly Graces. I thought he himself might have needed lessons in those graces after his rudeness to me. I offered him the handkerchief, which I supposed Lucie must have dropped a few minutes before. The surprising thing, to me, was this young man's proprietary air in the matter. But there were more surprises for me. My companion cried eagerly, "Louis! How good to see you this early! I have prepared my lessons in Court French and am quite ready to confound London and Royalty. Have you breakfasted yet? I could dine with you, and we might converse in French."

I saw how the sight of the tutor had completely transformed Miss Amanda's slightly heavy features, making her radiant and very nearly beautiful for that all too brief moment before the young man replied, obviously ill at ease, "I fear we have . . . I have breakfasted earlier, Mademoiselle Amanda. And I am now about to ride into town on an errand."

"For my stepmama, no doubt," said Amanda.

Her cutting reference to Lucie Dalreagh again carried great venom for a girl of her years; yet, I saw now that much of this hatred had its origin in female jealousy over the tutor himself.

Considering Louis Minotte, without seeming to do so, I thought this a very reasonable infatuation for a girl of sixteen or so. The Frenchman was extraordinarily handsome, quite as "beautiful" as His Lordship had described him in his joking way. The young man's melancholy dark eyes, his luxurious black hair and even features, when combined with an ivory pallor that seemed almost contrived in its purity, all would have done justice to that shocking Lord Byron. Somewhat amused, though I preserved a perfectly sober countenance, I could not acquit the young tutor of deliberately imitating the Byronic look.

Trying to avert what I could see was going to be another unpleasant mood in Miss Amanda, I said, "Your pardon, sir. I am Anne Killain, the housekeeper. If there is anything I can do to . . ."

The Frenchman bowed, but in a nervous way refused my offer. He seemed a very serious person, which doubtless was another trait that attracted a romantic-minded girl of Amanda's age, but I would have preferred at least a semblance of pleasant expression.

"Thank you, no. I fear this is a matter Madame has entrusted to me."

I ignored the affront, smiled and curtsyed, then started on, but I had lost my companion. Amanda stopped and said to Monsieur Minotte loudly enough for me to hear, "What is so urgent that Miss Killain cannot know of it and have it attended to? These errands should be run by the servants, Louis. I wonder what my delicate stepmother desires in the village that is so secret. Can it be a rendezvous?"

This was not the way to win the tutor's high regard, I thought, but he seemed disturbed by larger matters, for he indignantly disclaimed any romantic errand.

"You do me an injustice, mademoiselle. I have been asked to carry the former housekeeper's boxes and other property to her."

I would have gone on, but I was startled by the excitement in Amanda's voice.

"Louis! Have you seen her? Is she furious at her dismissal? She told me the last time I saw her that nothing could persuade her to go." Her voice faltered as though she feared she had said too much, and I was puzzled by the hesitant addition, "She . . . she was assisting me in . . . that is to say, she told me she had discovered something. A vital bit of evidence."

Louis Minotte cut in sharply in French. "Evidence of what? What is this evidence you speak of?" After a pause, during which Amanda seemed to be silently translating, he repeated his question in English.

By this time, she must have recovered her composure, for she was almost flippant as she answered, "Evidence that we truly have a Black Abbess—and that it was she who was seen in father's room the night he died."

"Amanda!"

His use of her name surprised me, but was quite clearly no surprise or discourtesy to the girl. The thing which really disturbed me was my awareness that her reply now had become no longer flippant, no longer a joke. She meant what she said.

"It's true, all the same. I used to think Old Herring told those silly ghost tales to alarm Lucie. I even added a few embellishments. But, Louis—since Herring left, I think I have seen her."

In a voice that revealed such obvious strain that I stopped and stared at him, Monsieur Minotte asked, "You have seen Madame Herrenrath? Here at Mist House?"

"No, silly! The Abbess! And the ridiculous thing is . . . now, no one will believe me. I told Uncle this morning, and he said I was become a bluestocking and must stop my reading of those horrid mysteries. But she is here, Louis, somewhere in Mist House. And I cannot make anyone believe me. Isn't it too absurd?" And she began to laugh.

I thought her laughter was very close to hysteria, and I turned back to see if I could not persuade her out of this mood. As for her other listener, I really thought the poor young man might faint, he looked so pale.

5

It was simple enough to separate the tense and unnerved pair. I merely asked Miss Amanda if I was headed in the right direction toward the household quarters, and she almost ran to join me, while the handsome Frenchman turned and walked abruptly in the opposite direction. It did not seem to me that this was the way toward the village of Dalreagh Dale, at whose bridge the night before I fancied I saw the lean shadow of the Black Abbess myself, but it was not my concern to play the turnkey with one of the gentry; so, I devoted my attention to my own future tasks as manageress of the household.

It had rather surprised me that no butler was employed; in the general run of things, I should have been in a position immediately beneath either that august figure or a steward. I mentioned the omission to Miss Amanda, who seemed less shaken now that we dealt with such mundane matters.

"The house belongs to Uncle, but since he is not married—he was jilted, nearly at the altar, by Mama—he lives here only on occasion. He allowed Papa and Mama and Grandpapa Wye to make Mist House their home. I was born here. In those days, we had a butler as well as a steward . . . But after Mama died, Papa let the steward go and managed the estate himself, even when he married that insipid Lucie. But ever since his accident, he spent a deal of time in bed. And then Uncle came up from London and took over the affairs."

"What sort of accident was it, miss?"

She shrugged. "Come along in. These are the stillrooms, and beyond are the kitchens. They lead by that little passage into the Great Hall. We do not dine, in the family, at the tables in the Great Hall, but just this side of it, in the old breakfast parlor. It is commodious and quite comfortable. The Hall has such intolerable drafts."

I looked at everything but could not help being very curious about the Honorable Kevin Dalreagh's "accident," which Lucie's letter to Miss Hunnicut had briefly mentioned also.

"Was your father injured in an accident on the estate?" I asked when the exasperating girl would not continue.

"Nothing of consequence. You cannot make a sinister plot of it. Old Herring and I both tried, but there was no one suspicious. No one to blame. Papa was riding to Dalreagh Dale beside the river early this fall, as he and Louis—

Monsieur Minotte—often did. He took a toss and got a broken arm and a few nasty bruises. Papa came riding back, cool as you please, with Louis. But of course, Louis was frantic. Papa had always been very good to him, and he felt responsible. Such nonsense! We all take a toss now and again. Every good rider does."

"And did Monsieur Minotte say nothing of the accident, the particulars?"

She had been about to demonstrate the new ovens which were installed within the huge, sooty, ancient fireplaces, but she straightened her sturdy back stiffly and looked at me, rather like a duelist who suspects a secret lunge.

"What do you mean? What could he say? Louis helped to support poor Papa in the saddle on the return. Father was in some pain, as you may imagine, and in a vile temper. In any case, Louis did all that was humanly possible. He even helped to set Papa's arm, for we could not get in a surgeon fast enough."

"I understand. Monsieur Minotte is an unexceptionable young man." It was the most innocuous thing I could say, but even this remark earned me a suspicious glance from her. She had been about to make an introduction and was waving to a stout, comfortable-looking woman of fifty or so, whom I supposed to be the cook, when I mentioned my opinion of the tutor. The stout woman laughed pleasantly, one of those breathy, fat laughs, and bobbed respectfully before Amanda could finish the introductions.

"Aha, Miss Amanda! Still another female who finds our Frenchie a true beau. He is like those Barbary pirate folk with his—what do they call it?"

Amanda did not like this at all. " 'Harem' is the word, Bess. And it's most improper of you to speak so of your betters. Besides, Miss Killain has no opinion of him whatever. Isn't that so, Anne?"

"Quite so," I agreed, smiling a little. "I have no opinion of Monsieur Minotte." This was an evasion but not a lie. I could, at least, assure the girl that I was no rival for the Frenchman's affections.

Amanda left me in the capable hands of Bess Kempson, who invited me to breakfast, during which time she presented most of the staff to me. There were fewer than I might have expected in so large a building, and I tried to remember them all, but it was patently impossible. Meanwhile, as I ate and casually questioned the cook about the house and its workings, I realized that it was entirely supported by the Earl of Dalreagh and that it was he who had the final vote on any household decisions I might make. Because I cared very much for his good opinion, I hoped I need not trouble that busy peer too much on trivial matters. I would try to learn all I could without annoying him.

For my first tour of inspection throughout all the upstairs chambers, I took Phoebe, the buxom, blonde, "screaming maid" whom I had encountered in the dark halls early that morning. I wanted to find my way about and to discover which apartments and sections of the building were in use. It would be absurd to lose my way in this labyrinth which was to be my charge and responsibility, and my reason for taking Phoebe was to reduce some of her trembling fits and to point out to her that the Black Abbess did not linger in every drafty place.

Almost at once, however, all my good intentions were undone. I had asked her to point out the apartments belonging to the various members of the family, including the Frenchman. These we would not enter until given permission, but I thought it necessary to have some idea of their situation and was anxious to learn what could be done about cleaning and refurbishing the better unused apartments. We had passed several closed doors when Phoebe said suddenly, "Ay, mum, there'll be an empty one. Or is it the next? Some is locked, as you may know."

"Faith now, we can only try them," I said, and as she nodded toward the nearest door, I tried the oversized, ornamental modern door knob. The door swung open into a gentleman's bedchamber, done in what I knew was the highest degree of masculine elegance. No need for Phoebe's wildest confusion to tell me that we had intruded on the apartments of His Lordship, the Earl, and that the room was inhabited by the gentleman himself. He was dressed for riding and being fitted into his spotless boots by his manservant.

I started to back out, silently praying that he had not noticed us, and almost succeeded in my escape before the Earl called out to me in that faintly amused voice I had already found both playful and disturbing. However charming it might be, I suspected that the musical quality would not be quite so enchanting if he were angry. There was, after all, behind that handsome and slightly amused face, a pride and hauteur that told me he was not a man to be made a fool of.

"Come in. Come in, Miss Killain. It isn't often these days that beauty comes to seek me out in my chamber, as it were. Now, in my younger days . . ." His shrug was humorously eloquent.

As he was scarcely thirty-five and quite the most attractive male I had seen since my husband's death, I took this to be a play for a compliment and refused to be drawn in. When I replied, very gravely, however, I found it impossible to hide the amusement in my eyes.

"As you say, sir. But a gentleman of Your Lordship's distinction and title will always be sought out by ladies of mature years and judgment."

The Earl raised an eyebrow and looked affronted.

"What a sting the wench carries, eh, Hobbs? We must be on our guard."

Though the sturdy little servant grinned, the Earl's remark shook that foolish Phoebe, who began to retreat still farther, curtsying incessantly and muttering "Not my fault, Y'Ludship. Indeed! Not my fault."

His Lordship waved her away impatiently.

"Hobbs, we have shocked the girl. Take her somewhere to recover. Miss Killain and I will make our own peace."

Hobbs obediently took Phoebe's arm and escorted her down the hall, more or less as if she were in custody.

I looked to see if the Earl had both boots on securely; for if there is one thing I learned long ago about the gentry, it is that no finger marks from inexpert persons like myself must ever soil the splendid gloss of those boots.

"I shock the natives," Richard Dalreagh said to me as he turned to finger his cravat, which had apparently not been arranged quite to his satisfaction, "but I am persuaded I do not shock you, Anne . . . That is your name, is it not?"

"Like you, sir," I said, "in my younger days I might have been, but scarcely at my present august age."

He laughed. "A touch. A touch, I do confess." He seemed to be intent on the precise and snowy folds of his neckcloth, but I caught his eyes suddenly in their mirrored reflection and knew that, for all his pretense, he had been watching me. I felt absurdly conscious under the gaze of those eyes and began even to regret my superior attitude toward poor Phoebe, for I understood now some of her own timidity. My hair had blown a bit in the drafts that prowled about the dark corners of Mist House. I was wearing a lilac gown quite as simple as yesterday's frock, and a trifle faded from age, and I wondered suddenly if he thought the square neckline too low-cut for my position, though no one had ever called it daring. Miss Amanda dressed more sedately, it is true, but I privately thought her choice of clothing was a great mistake in a girl of sixteen. Perhaps he considered that my Irish tongue made too free with my employer's dignity.

A trifle shaky in the knees, I curtsied and, remembering my place, said sedately, "By your leave, I will retire, sir." I started to leave but moved only two or three steps before he spoke.

He did not relieve my uneasiness when he replied with a crisp hauteur that stopped me in mid-step: "You are remiss in your duties, Miss Killain. I have not given you permission to go."

I must have looked utterly perplexed, because he beckoned to me with his forefinger, and I moved obediently across the room toward him.

"Yes, sir."

"Here. Do the impossible. Adjust this cravat without creasing it. No woman of my acquaintance has ever accomplished the task."

I reached for the many immaculate folds, aware at once of two very different sensations: my ability to accomplish what His Lordship called "the impossible" and my inadequacy to deal with his gaze, which I avoided but could not forget.

I kept my attention sternly on the white muslin, and whenever my thoughts wandered to the fine shape and set of Richard Dalreagh's chin or my eyes chanced to notice his mouth, which I found admirable, but far too close for my own self-assurance, I was disgusted that I could not remain calmly unmoved.

I finished my task, lowered my fingers and took one step backward, regaining my composure while he examined my handiwork in the pier glass.

"Excellent," he approved me. "I hadn't thought it possible." He put out his hand, stopping me with a casual, easy grip, and smiling. I was relieved at his smile, for it was gentle and humorous, not at all the usual lecherous grin with which a woman in my position was often favored by her lordly male employer.

"Where have you been this decade and more, Anne?"

His use of my name was overfamiliar, but I confess I did not remind him of this. I said quietly, "The world is a busy place, and there is always need of a housekeeper, sir."

He cupped my chin in his palm. I did not resist. Nor did I feel empowered to do so.

"Lucie tells me you are a widow. A very young one, I think. How does it happen?"

I must have shown in my countenance something of my feelings at this question, for I could not speak, and yet, he understood. Whatever he did in the future or however he might be concerned in the curious mystery at Mist House, I must forever recall these moments between us on that first day of my service at the ancient house. He withdrew his hand from my chin and gently, playfully touched my cheek.

"No matter. I see that it was not a marriage of convenience, as I had supposed." He paused. I thought he was about to let me go, and so he did, but not before he murmured, with none of his previous amusement, "Some men are fortunate. Others are merely . . . lucky."

Though I did not understand the distinction he made, I was deeply moved by this change in his voice and realized for the first time that his fortune, his title, his good looks all hid a surprising discontent, perhaps even an unhappiness. Womanlike, I laid this to the fact that he had never married. Then, I remembered the story his niece told, of his betrothal to Amanda's mother, and of how the girl, with what I considered lamentable taste, married his younger brother instead. I felt more drawn than ever to this "poor Lord Richard," who had the world in his breeches pockets and still could envy my husband, who was dead. My own awareness of the emotions this stranger aroused helped me to recover my careful, cautious other self.

"May I go, sir?" I asked, sensing that this moment should not be prolonged.

He laughed and withdrew his hand, as if my flesh burned him.

"By all means, Miss Killain. Go about your business of making this wretched heap a warmer, brighter place for the undeserving."

Embarrassed by the exaggerated emphasis on my presence, I looked toward the open door, a quick, instinctive motion that seemed to double what was, to me, his entirely inexplicable anger.

"Well then, go! What are you standing about here for? Go along!"

I hurried away in a tumult of confused sensations. For a few minutes, I had been dangerously close to feeling a physical attraction toward this Peer of the Realm, this man of such high station that even a lady might hesitate to fill her thoughts with him. As for a semi-servant in my position, a woman who had once been a scullery maid, he must possess an enormous charm to have held me in that spell even five minutes! Whatever the illusion I gave of careful propriety, I was well aware of the Polite World and the many social strata that comprise it.

I took a few moments to regain my composure and then returned to the servants' quarters and asked Bess Kempson to recommend for my guide, someone a little less given to hysterics.

"Nothing easier, miss," said the obliging cook as she paused in the midst of preparing a deliciously aromatic ragout. "I've my own boy, Jeremiah, that His Lordship put into training for a footman. He's been and come from the village to fetch spirits for Mrs. Lucie. The lady has the vapors."

"Oh, I'm sorry," I murmured, stricken with guilt at having delayed my respectful call upon her. "Does she suffer these vapors very often?"

Mrs. Kempson leaned forward over the deal table, shaking a carefully larded rabbit's hindquarter.

"Believe me, miss, there's ladies as gains their pleasure from the vapors. Have you heard? . . . she walks . . ."

"Walks?" I repeated, mystified. Then, I understood. "Yes, of course. She is a somnambulist. Perhaps she is troubled by something. She seems unhappy."

"Ha!" snorted forthright Mrs. Kempson. "Lazing away, more like, if you'll pardon the truth on it." Then, over her floury countenance, which was streaked with spices, came a beaming smile. "Jeremiah! This is Miss Killain that the staff was speaking of. You'll take your duties from her."

A lank, shy young man with wiry red hair made his appearance, dragging the small trunk of my possessions, which I had entrusted to a wagoner going north at even slower pace than the Accommodation Coach.

"For you, miss. Could I oblige by carrying the little box to your room?"

"Thank you. If you would be so—" I looked at Mrs. Kempson. "How absurd! I've no room as yet."

After a moment of bafflement, the cook had an idea which seemed perfectly simple to her.

"As to that, miss, you'd do best to see His Lordship. He'll have all straightened out proper in a trice."

This was one solution I would certainly postpone. After my odd meeting with him that morning, I should be fortunate not to find myself sleeping in the stillroom.

"I will not disturb him at the moment. But what of the previous housekeeper's apartment?

I think I might properly remove to those rooms, unless there are objections."

Red-haired Jeremiah looked at his mother, who shook her head ever so faintly. I caught that strange little exchange but understood I was not to have known of it.

"*Are* there objections?" I repeated, a trifle sharply.

"No, no, miss. None in the least," Mrs. Kempson assured me with breathless haste. "It is just that some of her boxes is still in place. She's not seen fit to send for them."

"But she has," I remembered suddenly. I motioned to Jeremiah. "Show me to the housekeeper's quarters, and then, I'll bring down my portmanteau from Mr. Kevin's chamber."

Jeremiah obeyed me without a word, and we were already on our way across the kitchen when Mrs. Kempson called to me in a tone that sounded ragged and strained, "When—beg pardon, miss! When did the other housekeeper send for her things?"

"Only this morning. The French tutor told Miss Amanda he was carrying the woman's boxes into the village."

"So that is how it was. I wondered."

But Jeremiah set my trunk down in a pool of chilly winter sunlight while he protested to his mother, "How can that be, Mama? The Frenchie passed me this morning, riding into the village. He was mounted on Mr. Kevin's mare.

He said to me that the mare was fresh and needed the exercise. But he'd no boxes by him. No cases nor ladies' bags."

His mother caught her breath. I wondered at the agitation of the two Kempsons but felt that I owed it to the Dalreaghs to practice discretion; so, I made a pretense of dismissing the matter that troubled these two.

"In any case, will you take me to Mrs. Herrenrath's former apartment, Jeremiah? Once I am situated, we can decide what best to do with the woman's property."

"Aye, miss." He shouldered my trunk handily, and we departed through the passage between the buttery and the small breakfast parlour.

"Old Herring—pardon. I mean to say, Mrs. Herrenrath had her rooms up on top story, in the front over the entrance hall," young Jeremiah explained. "So we've two ways. There, by steps the family uses, and there, over to the new wing toward the rear. You'll like them best, I'm thinking."

I assumed the boy knew his subject better than I and followed him up to the top floor, remembering with a smile the ridiculous, foredawn encounter between Phoebe and me on this flight of stone steps. I was surprised when we reached the housekeeper's two rooms in the front of the building. Although I had been prepared by the conversation of the Kempsons, the little sitting room did seem extraordinarily "occupied."

I was prepared to find two or three garments hanging in the clothespress against a side wall of the bedchamber and perhaps a knitted coverlet that was obviously the property of Mrs. Herrenrath. But the moment I stepped into the sitting room, I heard Jeremiah kick something out of his way as he set my trunk down upon the carpet. It was one of a pair of bed slippers with that comfortable look, as though they had for a long time accommodated short, broad feet. Similarly, there was a small, chime clock on the darning table beside a chair with a faded, petit point covering.

"Mrs. Herrenrath's clock," Jeremiah explained, seeing my interested glance. "The maids has told Mrs. Lucie of it, but she only says there'll be a call for it. We've but to be patient."

I could see everywhere the signs of my predecessor's existence while Jeremiah went about throwing open the dusty, mullioned windows and rattling shutters. I began to wish I had been placed anywhere but in these rooms, which seemed to carry the very breath of the unknown Rachel Herrenrath on the fetid air. The rooms themselves were pleasant, and the view of moat, small bridge, and watery, flooded countryside was an attractive one, even in winter. The brightness of the sun in the rain-washed sky made every object sharp and clear. I found myself thinking suddenly of a steel instrument which was always most dangerous when it was sharp and shining clear.

I started into the bedchamber and was surprised to find that the door beside the bed, which I imagined opened into the corridor, as did the one in the sitting room, actually opened on a narrow stone flight of steps that circles downward even into greater darkness.

"What is this?" I asked. "Not, surely, a secret passage. Or a priest's hole? One would think we were in the Middle Ages!"

However, the young footman seemed in no way disturbed. He stuck his red head into the gloomy place, saying cheerfully, "No, miss. It's quite new. Put here the last century. His Lordship's grandmama was a saintly lady. She had the steps put in so she might reach the old chapel directly below. It's forever being used when the housekeeper's gone. Not a bit of a mystery to it."

"I see." I did not like it, but at least there was nothing sinister about a flight of steps that led to a holy place. "I should think it a much quicker way to reach the ground floor than around about, the way we came."

"Aye. It is that. Poor lady! She had her precious steps all her life and finally died of them."

"How so?" I had suspected all along that the

pleasant, commonsense addition of these steps would have an unpleasant aftermath, and sure enough, the boy finished his tale with a shrug,

"When she was a very old lady and going down to her prayers with the aid of a walking stick, she caught her stick in the train of her bedgown and fell. Her young grandson Richard, His Present Lordship, that is to say, almost caught her. But it was no use. Poor old lady was stone dead, and so Master Richard came to be rich as a nabob." He grinned at me. "A bit of blood, as you might say, makes for a good tale, I always think."

"Thank you. That will be all," I said stiffly and started to usher him out by the chapel steps, but he excused himself, ignored the steps, and went out by the sitting room into the corridor.

I could scarcely blame him.

6

Fortunately, there was a very serviceable bolt on the door, and in a moment of exasperation, I slammed the bolt home, satisfying myself that no unexpected visitors, ghostly or otherwise, would be visiting me in the night from the chapel below. Then, I set about unpacking my trunk and placing my own property so that the two rooms would not so clearly show the presence of Rachel Herrenrath.

I was still busy at this when there was a brisk rap on the sitting room door, and when I opened it, I saw the Earl's sturdy little manservant, Hobbs, in the corridor, carrying my portmanteau. His highly colored cheeks puffed out like small red apples, and he appeared to have been hurrying.

"His Lordship give me orders. Most strict he was about it, mum. I was to see to any little comforts as you might express a wish for."

His expression of the Earl's wish pleased me more than I would have confessed to anyone, for ever since his curious change of mood earlier, when I inadvertently angered him, he was in my thoughts. I stepped aside and let Hobbs bring the portmanteau into the bedroom, where he set it down and looked around approvingly.

"Ye're a quick one, mum, to have got all your little pretties out so right and tight. Makes everything look quite homely, as you might say."

"You might," I agreed in a rueful tone, "but unfortunately, much of what you see belongs to my predecessor. I would prefer to have all her things removed, but I don't like to until I am given permission. I shall probably see Mrs. Dalreagh later today and ask at that time."

Two things happened at once in answer to my remark, and it was awkward that they occurred together.

Lucie Dalreagh called to me from the corridor all in a flutter.

"Are you here, Anne? How comfortable I shall be, knowing the household is in your hands and not that snooping Old Herring!"

She followed this flattering opinion by hurrying through the sitting room into the bedchamber just as Hobbs bellowed out candidly, "Shouldn't think you'd heed a word from that quarter, mum. It's the Master what makes all the rules hereabouts, not our frippery Mrs. Lucie. A sillier lady never lived, says my Lord."

In the desperate hope that my own voice would block out Hobb's rude observation, I cried out a welcome to Lucie, behaving in a loud, ostentatious way, which would certainly have surprised those who thought me calm, quiet, and dignified.

"Miss Lucie! Do come in. What a lovely set of rooms you have given me! I am just rearranging things a trifle. Hobbs was so good as to fetch in my portmanteau . . . Thank you, Hobbs. And thank your master. I am most appreciative of his kindness."

"Ay, mum!" He gave me a military salute, bowed to Lucie, and was about to depart by the chapel steps when he noticed that the massive door was locked. He grinned at me. "You needn't trouble about smugglers and cutthroats paying calls by this door, mum. There's a door opposite yours that opens into the Long Gallery. Anyone coming up here need not come to visit you. They can always step out yonder into the Gallery."

"Thank you. I am greatly reassured," I told him, heavily ironic.

But he only grinned and left by the sitting room door while Lucie fussed with the bolt on the door beside us and, having opened it, peered down into the darkness below.

"Would you believe it, Anne? That horrid woman used to sneak down these steps at night and go about spying on everyone, servants and gentry alike."

"Some of her things are still here," I said, pointing out the more obvious ones. "I should like permission to remove them to some place where they may all be together. She is sure to want this clock and some of the other items."

"Yes, yes, of course," Lucie agreed, as if she had not heard me. Her attention was distracted by the view out the window, and then I too heard the sound of hoofbeats on the bridge over the river-moat and went to see who was riding. I was surprised to see how handsome Miss Amanda looked in her black riding habit, with its severe, almost mannish cut, her thick hair bundled at the nape of her neck, and her straight set head crowned by a beaver hat.

I was surprised at Lucie's uncharacteristic interest in her stepdaughter until I saw the dark, slender young horseman riding along the estate road beside the river. Louis Minotte was looking down and did not see Amanda until she crossed the bridge and was facing him in the center of the road.

"Poor child!" murmured Lucie in a patronizing voice, as though from the heights of mature experience.

"Really, Miss Lucie? Why is that?" I could not resist asking.

But this was a field in which Lucie Dalreagh had long been a proficient. Even as a girl in her first year at Miss Hunnicut's, she had the same sweetly patronizing tone when speaking of the other students and any of the infrequent visits of the gentlemen to whom they were betrothed or whose charms they extolled to each other after the candles were snuffed.

"Oh, Anne. What an innocent you are. That poor girl adores Louis. She is forever trotting about, throwing herself in his way. Perfectly useless."

I had no particular reason to protect Amanda from her feathery little stepmother, but I could not help asking with a sardonic edge to my voice, "Why is it useless? Miss Amanda looks very handsome today. And she sits a horse exceedingly well."

Lucie burst into a light, tinkling peal of laughter, the kind that makes the hearer grit his teeth.

"Anne, you were never up to snuff. Ladies who wish to attract gentlemen never let themselves be 'handsome.' And Amanda is so assertive, so very masculine. Louis prefers quite a different sort of female. Very feminine, of a certain delicacy, of—" I looked at her, and she caught herself, with a flutter of small, ineffectual pink hands. "That is to say, all Frenchman are said to prefer the very delicate—"

"Not all Frenchmen," I said flatly.

She patted my arm. "Yes, but then, you were very special, and I'm sure that sort of thing doesn't befall every—"

"Housekeeper?"

"Oh, dear! I really am maladroit today. But

look. See them now. He is so ill at ease with her. She quite overpowers him."

Unfortunately, there was some truth in her observation. I kept wishing that either Amanda would fix her sights on someone more suitable to her nature or that Monsieur Minotte would learn to appreciate those excellent qualities that I began to observe in her. I could well understand how the arrival of a woman like Lucie might destroy Amanda's burgeoning confidence in her own femininity.

Lucie leaned out the window and called down. I doubt if Monsieur Minotte so far below us heard her voice, but he was obviously searching for a way to avoid the invitation Amanda had evidently issued to ride with her, for he kept looking up and around until at last his gaze encountered Lucie's. My companion waved to him and then, as an afterthought, to Amanda. He apparently needed nothing else in order to excuse himself from attending Miss Amanda. She had seen us but now avoided the window while she exchanged a few words with the tutor. With a perverse desire to see Lucie outdone, I hoped we would see them ride off down the estate road together.

Nothing of the sort happened, however. There was a bit of Gallic shrugging, hand waving, and other methods of saying adieu, after which Miss Amanda gave a stiff signal on the reins, passed the tutor, and rode off directly across the muddy fields. I gasped at the girl's recklessness but could not stand there watching the course of love while my own, less romantic affairs were still in a state of flux.

"Then I have your permission to remove Mrs. Herrenrath's property, Miss Lucie?"

Vaguely, she came back to my small problems.

"Whose property? Oh, yes. Louis knows. He has instructions from Rachel, that detestable creature. He placed most of her boxes in the cellars—we have a storage sector beneath the chapel—and then, he brings her things into the village when she requires them."

For some reason, this surprised me.

"Then Mrs. Herrenrath is in the village now?"

"Certainly. But it needn't disturb you. She was definitely dismissed. Why do you ask?"

"Merely because Monsieur Minotte said he was taking the woman's boxes in to her today but he did not do so."

She was just going into my sitting room but stopped, her slight, willowy form suddenly as stiff as her stepdaughter's sturdy body. She began to finger objects on the darning table.

"How would you know that, dear Anne?"

"He was seen going toward Dalreagh Dale." The matter was of no importance, and I went on to dismiss it quickly. "No matter. I will gather up her things and remove them to the cellar or wherever—"

Lucie had clumsily let fall a small china figure I brought over from France and now went down gracefully on her knees to recover the pieces.

"I'm so sorry. It was frightfully careless. I'll have it replaced for you at once."

I was forced to use that old, polite lie that I did not care, this sort of thing happens; but she persisted in her apologies until I had quite tired of the subject. As she was leaving, I remembered the matter that had been interrupted by the breaking of my little china milkmaid.

"With your permission, then, I will gather everything belonging to Mrs. Herrenrath and—"

"Yes, do. And notify Louis Minotte. He will take care of them for you. He is very capable, I assure you."

I thanked her, and, as soon as she had gone, set to work making a comfortable set of chambers for myself. Presently, I had quite a collection of Rachel Herrenrath's things, the chief part of which I placed in a large travel bag I found in the clothespress. This I decided to remove to the storage rooms in the cellar when time permitted. I set the box and the rest of the collection in a heap beside the closed and bolted door to the chapel steps.

The rest of the day was occupied with various matters that seemed to have accumulated for a very long time, even before my predecessor left. It was a joy to be really working again, and the more I worked, the less I thought of the past. Late in the afternoon, while Mrs. Kempson, the cook, and I were planning the menu to submit to Lucie for the following day, Miss Amanda came in, still wearing her stunning riding habit, to tell us not to lay the table for His Lordship.

"He is forever going off to London. If only he were not in the peerage, he could be something quite splendid."

I smiled at this notion. "I'm sure, miss, he is quite splendid even with his handicap."

She said seriously, "Yes, but he is so active in the House of Lords and has formulated some excellent legislation, but it's so difficult to get it sponsored, because, of course, you can't in the Lords." She added with pride, "I read nearly everything he does, you know."

Mrs. Kempson, on the sly, grimaced at me, but I pretended not to notice. I thought young Amanda's earnest concern with the problems of the world altogether admirable. Bluestocking, perhaps, but admirable.

"Miss Amanda," I told her sincerely, "I am sure His Lordship appreciates your interest and you knowledge of his work much more than—" I broke off in confusion, for we all, including Mrs. Kempson, knew exactly whom I meant.

The cook made a guttural, throat-clearing sound and brought matters back to the present situation.

"Beggin' your pardon, miss, but there's the table, the placing, you know. When His Lordship's away, Mrs. Dalreagh requests that the Frenchie–"

"Kempson!" Amanda interrupted thunderously.

"That is to say, the Monsoor sits in my Lord's chair. But you've set him by Miss Amanda."

"I see." I tried not to glance toward the girl but made the requested change.

When we looked around, Amanda was disappearing down the corridor, a lean, unbending black figure who suddenly looked much too old for her age.

"You mustn't think ill of Miss Amanda," the cook told me as she bustled around preparing the greater part of the present evening's courses. "She was always a trifle–well, less than pretty. She's a bit of her mama and a bit of her papa, the late Master Kevin. But it's the wrong bits, I'm afraid. Speaking of the face on her."

It was not a new theory, this notion of hers that one must make allowance for an intelligent female who was "less than pretty," but there were moments when I suspected Miss

Amanda possessed a more solid and normal foundation for the future than had Lucie Fairburn, for all of the latter's confidence in her own charms. I felt there was something about Lucie that was troubling, not her foolishness, nor her somnambulism, nor her obvious wiles where her stepdaughter's tutor was concerned, but the hidden cause of all these outward symptoms. Even the breaking of my china milkmaid was an oddity for the Lucie Fairburn I had known as a girl. The act was either unusually clumsy or the result of a severe attack of nerves. And Lucie was not a clumsy girl.

Dinner that day went very well, for which, of course, Mrs. Kempson and the staff deserved full credit. Nevertheless, I should have felt remiss if complaints had reached me afterward. I ate my own dinner in my charming little apartment, most obligingly waited on by Mrs. Kempson's red-haired son, Jeremiah, and by a young kitchen maid. I noted that to keep the contents properly warmed, they brought my tray up through the chapel steps, which startled me a little until I recognized their voices behind the wall.

When I opened the heavy door to them, I had to set aside Mrs. Herrenrath's property, and this reminded me that I had intended to remove the bags before the next day. I did not like to sleep with those reminders of my predecessor within sight of my bed.

"Is there a place nearby where these things might be stored?" I asked Jeremiah as he was leaving my rooms.

"Aye, mum. Beneath the chapel is where the Frenchie went and put Old Herrings trunk and a box or two, which was vastly oversetting to the staff because the Frenchie's not to do the work of the staff, you see." I said sympathetically that I saw and made a mental notation not to ask Monsieur Minotte to do any physical labor, including the removal of Mrs. Herrenrath's property. The boy, however, saw the difficulty into which he had placed himself and me, for he added apologetically, "I've been asked to do the boots of Miss Amanda and then to fetch up the hip baths for the ladies and Sir Peveril. But I could take them down tomorrow by dawn."

He was a pleasant boy and made the suggestion with an eagerness that was touching. I knew he wanted to impress the new housekeeper and understood the necessity for this. I had known such moments myself.

"No, no. I thank you," I said. "I'll attend to it myself. It shouldn't be far. These steps do have their advantages."

"That they do. But I'd be happy to oblige ir the morning, mum."

I refused his kind offer, and he went his way. I said nothing later when the girl removed my tray, but she surprised me when she left by the sitting room door instead of the quicker and more direct chapel steps. I was so curious, in fact, that I questioned her about it.

"Well, mum, if it please you," she murmured, curtsying shyly. "It's the little old gentleman, Sir Peveril Wye. He is forever in the chapel and the crypt below. It goes for to give me a fair bit of the shivers, seeing the little man pop out of the crypt of the chapel or wherever—when I'm alone and it's dark."

"Good heavens! I should think so. Thank you, Mavis."

The girl scuttled out. She had my sympathy, and I was glad she had warned me. I would thus be better fitted if I, too, came upon Sir Peveril unexpectedly. The business of the little man was odd, and I laid his continued presence here at Mist House long after the deaths of both his daughter and his son-in-law to some expressed preference by his granddaughter, Amanda. But I had not yet seen the two together, nor had I seen Sir Peveril with Lucie, his daughter's successor. Surely, there could not be much love lost there. Poor little man! Small wonder he spent his time in the family chapel and crypt.

Soon after the family had left the dinner table, I was forced by the exigencies of time to present the morrow's prospective menu to Lucie Dalreagh. I eventually found her in the music room, an attractive, many-windowed public room on the ground floor, where she sat working at a petit point firescreen but keeping a careful eye on the performance of Miss Amanda and her tutor, Louis Minotte. The Frenchman was rehearsing the proper Court Curtsy to her. I could scarcely believe this lumpish young woman, looking her worst in a pale blue, flowered, and frilled gown, was the same person as the proud, graceful equestrienne I had seen earlier on horseback.

I did not stay to see the resultant chaos, the shaming of a girl who obviously was not in her proper environment. I suspected she persisted in this program so that she might remain in the company of the handsome tutor. When I had received Lucie's approval of the menu, a vague and abstracted approval at best, I was leaving the room at once when she threw after me the curious remark, "Do not linger long in these halls, Anne. Remember the Abbess."

I went swiftly down the hall. I could still hear Monsieur Minotte fingering out a courtly tune on the pianoforte and counting in French, giving sharp orders as Amanda doubtless pirouetted, plunged again into a deep curtsy, and otherwise disported herself to her own disadvantage. There must be some way that the girl could be persuaded to live her own life and confine herself to the fields in which she displayed so well. However, it was not my affair, and I would only achieve the girl's contempt if I warned her that this pursuit of the tutor was destroying her own best qualities.

Despite my feelings, I was rather sorry when I got beyond the sound of those voices. The halls were inadequately lighted. I decided to speak to His Lordship about it when he returned. There was a candle sconce on the wall at the foot of the main staircase, and *it* had been lighted, but the drafty house made the flame an untrustworthy light to count on for very long, and at the top of those flights, there would be a long walk to the front of the house, where my rooms were. I saw a sheltered lamp at the end of the corridor, where it opened into the south portion of the Great Hall. It would be simpler to reach my rooms by the chapel steps to the corridor in front of my door. I had, of course, again bolted the door into my bedchamber. I needed but a single light, and I could reach my room much more simply by these chapel stairs, I thought.

I stopped by the stillroom, found a candle with a metal protector, and having lighted it at the fireplace, illuminated my way across the deserted Great Hall. I was used to the echoes now but liked them no better. The little improvised lamp cast every item in long shadow. I was unpleasantly amused when my own silhouette, cast high across the great stone wall, startled me momentarily.

After an examination, I made out the door between the Hall and the chapel. It was small and obscured by the darkness, but it opened easily, as if often used, and I stepped into the chapel.

7

It occurred to me as I entered the chilling stone chapel that if the place proved reasonably pleasant, I would bring Mrs. Herrenrath's things down that night, clearing them out of the way and giving me freedom from bothersome chores the next morning. I had no notion of wandering about empty chapels and crypts during the late hours of a winter night, but this place looked commonplace, unromantic, and I suspected, despite the servants, that it was totally lacking in mystery.

There was an altar, as was proper, on the easterly wall and, before it, a small prayer stand obviously retained from days before Henry the Eighth's snatching of the religious houses. Beneath the prayer stand and the altar, with its enormous wooden crucifix, lay faded purple carpeting that spread directly across the stone floor to an open stairwell, behind a cloister, with flights of steps winding downward, to the crypts, I assumed, and upward, undoubtedly past my bedroom. It was all perfectly harmless. Chilly, depressing, rather lonely, but harmless. I walked around the chapel, raising my candle to illuminate the high, time-darkened beams and the stained glass window, which appeared to have seen several centuries without cleaning. Aside from a great milord chair set against the far wall, the chapel was empty. The interior cloister lay shrouded in darkness, but I could see that it had been beautifully carved with an almost Arabic grace.

Being satisfied that there was no problem about the return to my rooms by this shorter means, I took a moment to examine the prayer stand and the chair. Both, as I had suspected, were thickly coated with dust. So much for the servants' tales told with fear and trembling. Nothing ailed the chapel but a lack of cleaning.

Nothing unbidden had been prowling about these regions during the night. It would take a phantom to dwell here without leaving his spoor in all this dust. Tomorrow, there would be a grand cleaning of all this region.

I crossed the chapel to the cloister and through the low arches to the steps leading upward. Once, I held the candle high to peer down into the stairwell. The way to the crypt was visible under my light as far as the archway into the burial place, where I could dimly make out a wooden door beside the archway. This would be the storage room with Mrs. Herrenrath's other things, no doubt.

I mounted the steps, hearing the scrape of

my own feet on the rough stone until I seemed to have climbed forever. Unlike the chapel, the steps were not dusty. They had been trodden a great deal lately, mostly as a shortcut by the servants, I assumed.

There were only three long flights to the steps upward, and when I found myself between two doors and at the abrupt end of the steps, with nothing but the distant roof over the stairwell, I guessed that the door on my left, which I tried and which was locked, must open into my bedchamber. I opened the door on the right and found myself in the Long Gallery. By this means, I entered my own corridor and sitting room within a minute or two. I gathered up Mrs. Herrenrath's property out of my bedchamber, later trying to balance it in one hand and arm so that I might carry the candle with the other. I wanted to have done with this tedious task as soon as possible.

By the time I was ready to return to the chapel and then, to the crypt, it was somewhat past ten o'clock. Though a small fire still burned cheerfully in my sitting room, giving some warmth to the bedroom beyond, I reached deep into the clothespress and threw around my shoulders what I supposed was my dark cloak. It would be drafty down among the tombs of ancient Dalreaghs, not to mention any unquiet abbesses.

This time, being assured of this simple way

to reach the ground floor of Mist House, I left by way of my own bedroom door. I started to hurry down the steps, but my bundles were heavier and much bulkier than I had expected, the cloth catching on several roughened stones, so that I had to make my way down the last two plunging flights much more slowly. My kid slippers, striking on each step, made echoing little clip-clop sounds that kept the air around me busy with the announcement of my coming. I was comforted by the very sounds which might have warned any listener; they also doubtless deafened me to alien noises.

I was pleased to reach the cloister between the stairwell and the chapel, where I paused long enough to catch my breath and, as I realized a few seconds later, to look about me. I did not wish to be unpleasantly surprised by Sir Peveril Wye in one of his nightly journeys to the chapel.

It would have been difficult for anyone, even a man as small as Sir Peveril, to hide himself in the chapel as the kitchen maid had indicated. Except in complete darkness, the big stone hall had only one conceivable hiding place, behind the altar. To satisfy myself and what I confess was the beginnings of a slight uneasiness, I crossed the worn stone floor over the carpet that Lord Richard's grandmother must have trod and raised my light above the altar. Nothing was there. Even the usual coat of dust was absent. Perhaps the little man really did hide there sometimes to frighten susceptible kitchen maids.

Satisfied that I was alone, I returned to the steps and started down toward the crypt, hefting one of the bundles as I used to heft the laundry for the workhouse in Dublin when I was a child. In doing so, I dropped a muslin nightcap out of the loosely tied bundle of Mrs. Herrenrath's things and looked down the steep, unguarded side of the steps to make sure where it landed. That matter was easy. It fell almost in front of the door which I assumed opened into the storage room. But my candlelight caught the faint, almost imaginary suggestion of movement just within the shadow outside the archway that led to the crypt.

My nerves seemed to tighten. I kept the sheltered candle carefully within the range of the steps and peered over the side again into what was not quite perfect darkness. A faint light existed in the great hall called the crypt, a place which was beyond the illumination of my own candle. I supposed that, somewhere, there was an opening to the out-of-doors. Again, however, I was in time to catch movement, a wrinkled hand very much alive clutching at the archway. I guessed, of course, that it was that tiresome little man, Sir Peveril Wye, and came on down the steps. But I took care to keep a tight grip on the handle of Mrs. Herrenrath's small trunk, which would make a sturdy weapon if hurled with all my strength. I persuaded myself that I was not so much nervous as indignant. This was helpful. Indignation carries its own strength.

At the bottom of the steps, it was much colder. There was a kind of damp miasma there, and I was glad I had the foresight to provide myself with a shielded candle. Even so, the flame wavered, and for a second or two, my heart wavered with it. When the orange glow rose again, I could see in addition to the old gentleman's wrinkled hand both his feet in bed slippers, and I called out, in the strongest voice I could manage in the circumstances, "Sir Peveril! You'll be catching a very nasty cold if that is your wish."

He shuffled out into the light of my candle, behaving in a cowardly way that made me feel quite leonine.

"Oh, dear girl, how glad I am to see you. I heard something . . . Come nearer."

I did so, struggling not to look over my shoulder. As it was perfectly obvious that the terrified little man was harmless, I set down the bundles and took his arm.

"Are you well, sir? May I assist you?"

He put his face horridly close to mine and whispered, "I've been coming into the chapel, you know, to catch a glimpse of her."

I was not sure I understood him. "I beg your

pardon, sir. A glimpse of—her?" I had some notion he was speaking of Rachel Herrenrath. "In the chapel?"

"But where else would I see her—the Abbess?"

I was very much inclined to dismiss this as pure fustian, but when I looked into his eyes, their darting, nervous pupils were a contagion. I, too, felt the edge of terror until I became aware of what he was doing to me, perhaps all unconsciously. Then, I tried to lead him away from the entrance of the crypt, but he peered around my shoulder, pinching my cloak and my arm in his effort to cling to me. Despite the freezing cold, his face was beaded with sweat. I could scarcely believe that this was all sham, a little game of his to keep occupied and perhaps let the household feel his special distinction.

"I tell them, but they do nothing. Not Richard nor the Frenchman, nor Amanda. And the Fluttering One merely—flutters."

I rightly assumed that the Fluttering One was his daughter's successor, Lucie Fairburn.

"Come along, sir," I told him, treating him with the mixture of deference and firmness that has always proved successful with the young people in my charge. It was a trifle annoying to think I must spend a portion of each night delivering this little leprechaun to his bedchamber, but I intended to get my own work completed down there that night in spite of my knightly friend. I was not sure even then, as I coaxed Sir Peveril toward the steps, why it was so important to me that Rachel Herrenrath's property should be completely removed from my sight.

He looked back as, with my help, he mounted the steps.

"I meant to wait in the crypt, but I lacked the nerve. Do not tell them. I could not face her down."

"I understand. You are afraid of the crypt; so many ancient dead. But it is quite safe, sir. Monsieur Minotte comes down often to take things to storage. Miss Lucie tells me he does this, and he is not afraid. The crypt cannot hurt you. Come, now . . . one step more. And another. You shall wait in the chapel, and then we will go together through the dark corridors."

"Now, pretty miss, now! We mustn't wait." He was shaking badly, and I wished I had some good brandy with which to ease his chills as well as to build his courage.

"Why not, sir? Only a moment. Two, perhaps. Just sit quietly in that chair. I shall join you as soon as I have placed Mrs. Herrenrath's things in safety for her. That little room beside the crypt is the storage chamber, is it not?"

He was tugging away from me, not nearly so reassured as I had hoped he might be. He looked all around, even into the unlighted corners of the ancient chapel.

"Please, my child, someone must believe me. *She is here*. It was she who murdered Kevin. I suspected then, but I could not prove it. I thought if I confronted her, I might . . . but I am a coward." He shuddered.

Despite the old-fashioned black silk coat he wore, his bony shoulders looked pitiful, hunched and pulled together as though he hoped to make a smaller target of himself.

I was furious at my own cowardice when I glanced up and then studied each corner as he had, half expecting to encounter the unfortunate man's phantom. He seemed inordinately pleased that his fear had been conveyed to me, and his little prehensile fingers jammed at me to punctuate his understanding that I shared those terrors.

"You do fear her. You must not confront her tonight, my dear. I am old. One night, I shall take courage and do so. That is why I try each evening, in the hope that this night, or the next, will make me brave. But not . . . tonight." He looked into my face with a smile whose poignance touched me. "I wish to enjoy a few more days. The days can be excessively pleasant, you know."

I had to be brisk and sure for both of us. I knew that. Anything else would send him into panic again.

"Of course. Sir Peveril, you will do as I ask, will you not? You must remain here until I return. You must not be wandering about these halls without a lamp. You do understand."

He raised his head with every sign of indignation.

"Perfectly, my dear child. I am not senile." I reddened at this very proper setdown. He added, confiding, "I had a lamp, you know, when I started into the crypt. But I dropped it, and it died—and I grew afraid."

"Very well. I'll fetch it up for you when I've done."

About to leave him, I wanted very much to repeat my warning, but one look at his stiff yet quivering chin told me he would resent the repetition. Hoping for the best, I saw him huddled in the great chair and went across the chapel to the steps, hearing no sound behind me but my own feet as I moved off the carpet onto the icy stones. I knew exactly what I would see when I turned around before going down the steps: little Sir Peveril, crouched there like an ancient child, the pupils of his eyes darting back and forth and from side to side, as if impelled by some strange terror all their own. Sir Peveril was left with no light but the faint glimmer of the stars through the stained glass window. Thinking about him there alone in the chapel, I hoped this was enough light for the little man.

It was quite simple, descending the steps again toward the crypt and the storage chamber. I had done this scarcely minutes before, only to find that the creature whose presence sent me into a shiver of apprehension and whom I had watched with hawklike vigilance was this innocent old man whose fears I hoped I had just allayed.

By the time I reached the level of the crypt and the chamber, I was calm again, disturbed only by the knowledge of Sir Peveril's insensate fears, which I had not yet proved, to my own satisfaction, were entirely false. I found all of Mrs. Herrenrath's property where I had left it in piles on the great stone blocks that composed the floor of the passage outside the crypt. The door of the storage chamber being immediately at hand, I took out the ring of housekeeper's keys assigned to me and tried those which seemed likely to fit the lock.

It was exasperating to discover that none of my keys suited, and I was beginning to wonder if the key to this small room had been deliberately omitted, when one key which, I could have sworn, would not fit, managed to open the lock by the sheer pressure of my fingers. Within was nothing but a large closet with a number of trunks, portmanteaus and bandboxes. I raised my candle and looked farther to reach such labelling as was visible upon the various boxes, bits of paper bound to the boxes with thin cord, and other such contrivances.

It was astonishing. Each of the pieces of luggage was carefully labelled with the name of Rachel Herrenrath. I could scarcely believe that she had left so much property behind her. Surely, this was the accumulation of a lifetime. Boxes, trunks, small bundles . . . I tried several, opened those that were unlocked, and found clothing, shoes, and black hose, all of a divergence in style reaching back ten years to that period when I was barely out of childhood, working and learning at Miss Hunnicut's instructions. I saw such articles as well which Mrs. Herrenrath must surely have found useful every day, including a pair of glass squares that undoubtedly were her spectacles. Or was she so rich that she owned two pairs? The only explanation I could reach was that she expected to return to Mist House when I was gone.

Having set my own additions to Mrs. Herrenrath's property in this small, dark chamber, I stepped out and closed the door, still deeply puzzled at this collection of a lifetime's effects, all neatly gathered in one room in a house which, presumably, she was never again to enter. Freed now of the burden of her belongings, I raised the candle once more, always aware of whispering sounds, as though another creature besides myself walked over these stones and had walked over them while I remained in that closet. I looked out and up the steps to be quite sure I was still alone in this eery place.

I was about to start up the steps when I recalled my promise to locate Sir Peveril's lamp where he had dropped it within the archway entrance to the crypt. With a certain reluctance that shamed me, I turned and went back to the arch where I had first encountered the little man that night. I looked about, but the lamp was not there.

The room of the crypt was much larger than I had supposed, a rectangular stone hall with one barred opening to the night sky near the roof over the south wall. It was the various burial places themselves, however, that fascinated me; for I had not supposed the tombs would be neatly placed in rows on the stone floor, some with exquisitely carved likenesses of the bodies within on the coffin lids. All of these were eery enough, but most truly terrifying was the series of life-size statues standing sentinel in no particular order about the hollow, icy place.

The very first of these statues represented a saintly female in the severe habit of some kind of *religieuse*. For one horrible minute, I thought this was the Black Abbess. I was so struck by this figure's resemblance that I went over to it to make examination and also to pick up a lamp, which I assumed was Sir Peveril's, and which had rolled to the feet of the stone *religieuse*. The statue was remarkably lifelike, as were, apparently, the other tributes to ancient departed members of the Abbey: all female, as nearly as I could make out by the flickering light of my candle, which cast everything, every coffin and every statue, in its own elongated shadow. But this, of course, was not the Black Abbess.

I must have spent more time than I intended in this strange place with its little company of dead nuns and lay sisters, because the candle flame bent and wavered, and I thought with a chill that it was burning down, but the flame soon sprang up again. It had only been a sudden draft, after all. Having come this far into the center of the stone army, and being assured of the life of my candle, I lingered with a perverse curiosity to see if one of these long dead sisters had had the distinction of presiding over the Abbey. It seemed to me, as I examined each in turn, that somewhere among them I had seen a statue of an abbess, though hardly likely to be that abbess who had profaned her vows in the arms of the neighboring Lord of Dalreagh.

One by one, I lighted the gaunt stone figures; and then, as my candle was raised still another time, throughout the chapel and crypt there was the most unearthly cry, so hideous, so unnatural that I thought for an instant it must come from a trapped animal of some kind. Then I remembered little Sir Peveril huddled upstairs in that great chair and probably terrified for his life. Undoubtedly, the scream was his. He had been frightened by a sudden draft of air or the movement of a tapestry in the ancient room. I hurried across the crypt among all those weird statutes, whose empty eye sockets seemed, despite their emptiness, trained upon me.

8

By the time I started up the steps, I was beginning to worry about Sir Peveril's nerves. It might be perfectly true that he was safe in the physical sense, that no one had been within that chapel when I left it only minutes before, but unquestionably, his nerves were all a-tremble. His fears were based on a powerful imagination, even senility perhaps, but a fancied terror might prove fully as dangerous to a man of his years and sensibilities as a real terror. I began to run. At the top of the steps, I paused momentarily, remembering that I had left the little man in semidarkness, the great chapel illuminated only by the starlight that sifted through the dusty bits and pieces that made up the stained glass window.

When I held the candle behind me, I began to make out the different objects in the chapel through a light that seemed faintly blue from my vantage point. Nothing moved, except Sir Peveril across the floor. He had either tried to rise from the high-backed milord chair or had fallen out of it and was *crawling* over the stones like an animal, his clawed fingers reaching for the warmth of the worn, purple runner of carpet before the altar.

"Sir!" I cried out, holding the candle high so that he was no longer in the sinister dark, "Let me help you. Don't move. You will make yourself ill if you are not careful. Now then . . ."

Rushing across the floor, I set the lamp on the altar and knelt to take his hands and stop those desperate, aimless movements of his.

"What is it? Why have you done this? Look at me, sir. Tell me!"

Close to him this way, I saw the dreadful strain on his body. The chords in his terribly thin neck stood out and the veins, thick and blue. He looked like a man in an apoplexy, his eyes starting from their sockets as he clung to me.

"Run, girl! She was here. She—" His lips worked painfully, his swollen tongue trying to pronounce the dreadful cause of his attack. "I thought . . . I thought—"

"Yes? What was it, sir? I am here. I will not leave you."

"No! Must run . . . run!" He crumpled against me, his body twitching in these, the last seconds of his life, and then he was still, the awful, bulbous eyes glaring at me, as if beseeching me to understand the words his tongue could not form.

Shifting his weight, I tried to set him with

his back against the altar, and while I was doing this, a shadow crossed the old man's face, the shadow of some one behind me, approaching the altar. So much shaken by fear and dread that I could scarcely hold Sir Peveril upright, I moved my head stiffly to look over my shoulder.

Just at first, before I could get a grip on my own terror, I thought the Black Abbess stood there, looming over the dead man and me. Slim, black-clad Louis Minotte was staring at Sir Peveril.

"Has he hurt himself, mademoiselle? I heard his scream. He is forever wandering about, risking injury in the dark."

"There need be no more fear of that," I said stiffly, with some bitterness. "I know death when I see it."

"Death! Surely, he is not dead. But only a moment since, I heard—"

"He was *frightened* to death."

The Frenchman bent over to examine Sir Peveril, and I felt, from his standoff manner, that even this contact with a dead body made him squeamish. I could scarcely blame him, and yet, I did. One must overcome such feelings, at any cost.

"What? But, mademoiselle, this is absurd! Where were you when he was so frightened?"

"I was in the crypt, or very near it. In the

storage chamber with Mrs. Herrenrath's boxes. I left them there."

He did not look at me, and I sensed that he was avoiding a face-to-face confrontation. For some curious reason, his pallor had deepened, partly from the discovery of Sir Peveril's body, but more, I think, at my last words. I could not pretend to understand this reaction. I had said nothing amiss, so far as I knew.

"Will you go and fetch someone, or shall I?" I asked, trying to prompt him to some kind of action.

He started, looked at me in confusion, and stammered, "Y-yes. It is so. I must inform Madame Dalreagh. It will be a most terrible shock. Madame is so fragile. She must be informed in such a way that—"

"Monsieur," I cut into this absurd excess of caution, "I shall remain with Sir Peveril, if that is what you are trying to ask me. When you have performed that delicate task with Mrs. Dalreagh, will you be so good as to inform Miss Amanda that her grandfather has just died of a fright?"

He was getting to his feet when I said this, and he looked at me in such a way that I could not acquit him of plain, unadorned cowardice—just when I needed a man of courage and, above all, of common sense. What a dreadful coincidence that this should happen only hours after Richard Dalreagh had gone from Mist House!

"Mademoiselle, that is to say, Miss Killain, what can you mean? The old Monsieur has died of a failure in the heart, is it not so?"

"He was frightened when I saw him first this evening. I left him there in that chair, and minutes later, I heard him cry out. He was crawling away, I think, trying to escape from . . . something."

He had recovered somewhat, his color returning as he asked, after moistening his lips, "Then, he did not immediately die? Was he of a condition to speak?"

"He believed he was confronted by the creature you call the Black Abbess."

We were both thrown into the shivers by a disembodied voice somewhere in the darkness of the chapel cloister. It took me no more than a second or two to recognize that gasping moan as the betrayal of Lucie Dalreagh's presence.

"Dear God, no! It was an accident . . . an accident!"

"Ma chère! Do not come nearer," Monsieur Minotte pleaded, and then, as I turned around, angry that I should have allowed myself to be startled by the girl's sense of drama, the Frenchman strode across the chapel. I stared at them, wondering if they would be bold enough to embrace in the presence of the dead, but Lucie, at least, recovered enough to put her hands up,

palms out, the pale flesh looking ghostly in the dark, as she warded off her protector.

"Tell her it was an accident, Louis. Not . . . what she thinks."

I got up. It was no use. The two of them, shivering and shaking, had begun to speak together, each urging the other to be calm, that all would be well. My knees felt odd, cramped and stiff, and when I moved, they were so weak I scarcely knew them for my own. I rushed past that foolish, ineffectual pair, as I conceived them surely to be, and out through the Great Hall to the lighted corridor, where I called for Mrs. Kempson and Jeremiah.

The cook, being naturally an early riser, had already retired, but I was intensely relieved to see her lanky, red-haired son, Jeremiah, who came running out, dragging a huge metal hip bath.

"Coming, mum. Coming. I've the water yet to finish heating."

"Never mind. Jeremiah, something has happened to Sir Peveril. We must send to London for His Lordship at once. Tonight. Who is the best person for this?"

"I'll go, if you like, mum. But it best be quick, for there's the fast Mail Coach from Lincoln to catch at Dalreagh Dale. It'll be passing afore midnight." He set down the hip bath but paused in a muddle, as well he might be.

"Beggin' pardon, but wouldn't a surgeon be of use?"

"He is dead. But we must have the persons to lay out the gentleman properly and to . . . prepare him. Do you know who that might be?"

"Aye. Just so. But there wasn't anyone for to lay out Master Kevin, savin' us here. So Mrs. Kevin, she done fair brave to do for her husband. You'd not think it of Mrs. Lucie. And Mama, she did the winding sheet."

"Never mind," I cut him off. "Are you sure you know where to find the Earl, once you reach London?"

"But mum, His Ludship spends the night at an inn 'twixt here and London. He's like to be there, and the Mail Coach fetches up there some-ut afore dawn."

"Good. If there is a surgeon in the village on your way, send him here. I'll fetch you enough money for your trip."

He started off on the run, and I blessed him silently for his quickness. I was discovering that this was not altogether a common quality. I hurried back to the chapel, where I found that the Frenchman and Lucie were kneeling beside the old gentleman's body, and as I approached them, I remembered suddenly an extraordinary comment by Jeremiah.

Was it possible this fragile, delicate Lucie Fairburn Dalreagh had actually prepared her husband for burial? Surely, I had misunderstood. Miss Amanda might have done so. She seemed an eminently capable girl. But I found it utterly incredible that the Lucie I knew, the Lucie of tonight's behavior, possessed strength of that sort—and strength it took to prepare a body for burial, as I well knew from experience.

After a minute or two of consideration, I persuaded myself that Jeremiah had used Lucie's name by accident. Undoubtedly, he had meant to say Amanda.

When I came nearer, I heard Lucie crying in low tones of desolation, "What am I to do? It must have been an accident. He cannot have seen— It was all settled. You know it was, Louis. Why would that Thing hurt him? Everyone persists in saying there is no Abbess. Well then, how are we to explain this? They have told him times without number. And yet, he persisted in these night wanderings, despite all I have done and you have done, to stop it."

Monsieur Minotte shook his head in the slow, perplexed way that warned me again that I would be hard pressed indeed to count on aid from him. I was surprised, however, when he said something to her in a very low voice and she looked over her shoulder at me. So he had known I was approaching all along. The strange woman had not shed a tear, despite all her fluttery concern for Sir Peveril. I assumed from this that her anguished behavior stemmed from some other fear, some other sorrow or panic that swept her to these terrors. Perhaps she *had* come to believe in the reality of the Black Abbess, as an apparition that truly haunted the house. I had heretofore supposed, when she mentioned it, that it was her way, as in the old days, of taking the products of imagination and life, mingling them together, and professing to believe in the conglomerate whole.

I told her now what had been done and got a severe setdown for having ventured out of my own province as housekeeper. Lucie would never speak with force or authority, but she reproached me in that wavering, slightly high-pitched voice of hers which served her quite as well but which irritated the ears much more than an out-and-out scolding.

"Anne, you have taken a great deal upon yourself in acting so quickly, sending the servants off, stopping my brother-in-law, who has important legislative work in London. All this could have been managed with more decorum by Monsieur Minotte and me."

"But miss—but madam!" I protested, aghast at this wholly unlooked-for reaction. "These things must be seen to at once. And since nothing was being—" I broke off, knowing how impossible it is to lay any blame at the door of one's employers. "That is to say, sure now, you'll be wanting a surgeon or someone in to examine the gentleman, to see if, conceivably, there is another cause of death."

"Perfectly true, Anne, but it is not your place to—to—" She waved her hand helplessly.

How curious, I thought. Her big, pale eyes are dry as bone . . . She is worried, nervous, but not in the least moved otherwise . . .

"I quite agree with you, madam," I said in a cold, clipped voice that did not sound natural to my own ears. "It is not my place to send for His Lordship. And I shall so inform Lord Richard when he arrives."

Lucie turned to the Frenchman again, torn by some emotion I could only guess was fear. "Oh, Louis! What is to be done? He will be frightfully angry and make a monstrous scold at me."

But by this time, he seemed more in control of himself.

"There, there, Luc—madam . . . We must be brave and do what we can with Miss Killain's help. Miss Killain can be very useful. You remember, you said that when you wished to replace Rachel. You said you could count upon your Anne, as you called her. Recall, my dear. Please do recall and be warned."

I wondered what that last word might mean. But under this male consolation, she recovered rapidly and put her hand up to me coaxingly. It was just as she used to do at the school, and though we were vexed with her in the old days as now, we always ended by being mollified into good humor again.

"Dear Anne, do forgive me. I was out-of-reason cross with you, and I must not be. You did your best. You tried to help me."

"Tried" indeed, I thought, not thanking her for her patronizing dismissal of the only things I could have done. I nodded to her a bit stiffly, and when Jeremiah came, booted and dressed for the road, I told him to speak to Mrs. Dalreagh for his instructions. A bit meanly, I also let him ask her for money with which to make the journey, and after considerable discussion between her and the tutor, she told me to fetch down her little box of household moneys from its special hiding place in her room.

"Rachel was used to care for the household expenses," she told me indifferently as she waved me on my way. "But Richard said that it would be quite in order, and good experience besides, if I were to have the handling of it."

It was possible that she might learn useful talents for her future as mistress of this house, I thought, if she did handle the moneys, and I went to obey her, but hoping she and Monsieur Minotte would soon have the body of the old gentleman removed to some place where it might be laid out. He looked so very pitiful, huddled there by the altar, an old and discarded heap, no longer even the chief subject of discussion among us.

By the time I returned with the box of silver, it was too late. Jeremiah had been sent on his way, with what suggestions countermanding mine I could only guess, and even there, I was not so much concerned about the instructions themselves as about the "why" of them.

"Never mind, dear Anne," said Lucie, as though she felt the need of placating me. "Monsieur has been good enough to provide the money, and the boy is gone. The sooner the better, don't you agree?"

I replied politely, but the truth of it was that Jeremiah's departure did not relieve me nearly so much as the fact that Sir Peveril's body had been removed to his bedchamber by the tutor and one of the footmen. There, Lucie informed me, we need do nothing until after dawn, when the surgeon would have arrived.

I *was* greatly relieved and, after gaining Lucie's permission, went up to my rooms and to bed. The previous night's slumber having been badly broken by my late arrival and then the prowling of Sir Peveril Wye, I hoped, despite the appalling event in the chapel, that I might sleep undisturbed; and so it was. For an hour, I lay there in this small, comfortable chamber where my predecessor had slept, puzzling out the mysteries of this house, and then went off to sleep and did not wake up until a bright sunrise had blazed on the winter landscape outside the south windows and so, by indirection, reached my rooms.

The little fire in the grate had long since burned out, but a few minutes after my awakening, Phoebe, the plump and nervous blonde maid, left my tray of morning tea outside the sitting room door, and it went far to restore warmth and comfort to me. Shortly after I had dressed, I was told to report to Sir Peveril's room, where the village surgeon, a brusque and capable little Scotsman, ordered me to assist him with the preparation of the dead man.

"Mrs. Dalreagh informs me that you are a capable lass, though I take leave to doubt it. You've the look of one better suited to pleasing the male gender," he said with what I could only consider embarrassingly brutal candor. I felt that words would be useless to disprove his first impression and went to work at once on the bathing of the dried and shrunken corpse. He eyed me from under grizzled brows and added the reluctant rider, "But no doubt, you can't help the Irish look of you."

Late in the morning, by the time we had finished our distasteful work, we were old friends, Dr. Malcolm and I. As he was departing, after arranging for the burial in the Dalreagh graveyard west of Mist House, Lucie sent word that she would be sleeping, under the effects of the laudanum he had left her, and I walked with Dr. Malcolm outside Mist House in the fresh and welcome sunlight. There was a stiff wind blowing, and my hair and ankle-length pinafore whirled around me like catherine wheels, but I felt refreshed after the forbidding hours within the stone monument to the past.

I walked with the surgeon to the coachhouse, where I found one of the boys employed as a groom. He fetched out Dr. Malcolm's old mare, and I saw the two of them off across the bridge and down the estate road—the stringy, indomitable Scot and his match, the lean and stringy mare.

I hated to go back indoors at that moment. Although my own uneasiness about the house might be explained away as the fantasy of ghostly Black Abbesses, and the contagion of the fear that made Sir Peveril die from no physical cause, I was reinforced in my feeling by Dr. Malcolm's last word to me. He looked up and scowled at the enormous stones that compose the Abbey facade of Mist House.

"Mark me, lass, you're not long for that accurst place. Get you gone before your cheeks lose that bonny color."

I had asked quite seriously, "Do you believe there truly is a ghost, Doctor, and that the old gentleman saw it?"

He looked down at me in his gruffly kind way.

"I believe old Wye saw something. Quite possibly an abbess. But I'll wager the Honorable Kevin did not 'see' an abbess. From all accounts, he died noisily, unpleasantly—poisonously." He gave his mare the signal to start, adding to me as the distance between us increased, "But I cannot be sure. I was in Lincoln at the time, and there was no surgeon to make examination. Good day to you, lass."

Yes, I thought, there is room for suspicion; but suspicion of what?

9

I crossed the little bridge and stood a few minutes, mesmerized by the churning brown waters of the river, guessing from its cocoa color that this was the debris of a storm higher up in the hills beyond. I had a strong desire to follow the path beside the stream, beyond the Dalreagh family graveyard, eventually climbing into those purple hills that were closer than they appeared to be. However, there were my duties in the household, and my responsibility to those who had employed me.

So, it was with reluctance that I returned indoors, going at once to the kitchen, where Mrs. Kempson and two scullery maids were busily at work baking what the stout cook called "funeral meats," although she was muttering about graveyard drunkenness and disrespect to the dead.

" 'Tis ever the same," she told me as I wrapped my hands in cloths and removed the spiced bread loaves from the ashes of the huge fireplace. "In York, they call it 'arvils,' but it's only an excuse for to drink themselves under the table, and all in the name of that poor, wee gentleman. Though how he come for to lie down and die, all alone in that wretched chapel—well, miss, it's more than I know."

Her words seared me to the heart.

"Don't. Please. If I had not left him alone in the chapel, he would be alive now." It still seemed incredible, and I protested vainly, against my own self-reproach, "I was only gone such a short time."

She looked at me in surprise.

"Eh? Where did you go, miss?"

"Sir Peveril had dropped his lamp in the crypt during his wanderings. I went down to get it and to put Mrs. Herrenrath's property in the storage chamber."

"Miss! You never!" She dropped a carving knife, which barely missed stabbing her instep. As she stooped and with some little creaking effort picked it up, she shot me a nervous side-glance. "Horrid place, isn't it? With all them dead nuns and such. I tell you flat out, miss—" She pointed the carving knife at me for emphasis. "I wouldn't no more go into that crypt at night than I'd fly to the moon." She brought the knife down on the meat, then looked at me from under her brows. "What . . . was it like? Did you seen anything . . . different . . . in them awful tombs and stone statutes?"

"I don't really know," I confessed. "I thought, for a few seconds, that something, one of the figures might . . . well, I felt something eery, but very probably it was nothing. Sir Peveril was above me in the chapel, and it was he who saw whatever frightened him to death." I seemed to relive it in the telling and thought with a deep, painful knowledge of my own part in his dying . . . *I* left him alone in that cold, dark chapel, knowing how afraid he was, knowing he had already seen something strange and sinister. Even by the most generous standards, mine was the neglect.

In order to avoid these thoughts, which interfered with the efficiency of my work, I asked Mrs. Kempson suddenly, "Have you made use of the storage chamber beside the crypt of late?"

She rolled dough in preparation for savory meat pasties and paused momentarily.

"Why are you asking, miss? What's in that chamber?"

"So far as I can see, nothing but Rachel Herrenrath's things."

"Ah!" But she said nothing further on the subject until I was leaving the kitchen to arrange for the cleaning of the guest chambers. Then, she started several times to say something and finally blurted out: "The staff—we did not like her, you know—that Herrenrath woman. Mark me, miss! She was forever prying and spying, and if it comes to that, she'd a deal of business with that horrid crypt."

I thought she stressed this entire matter of the housekeeper's prying and spying a trifle too much, and I asked her to her face, "Do you believe I will pry and spy, Mrs. Kempson? There is such a fine line between efficiency and spying."

Mrs. Kempson's plump face was flushed, whether from the fire or my blunt question, I did not know. As I watched, her lips set in a hard line, not like the fat, friendly features I had begun to think I knew.

"Well, miss, that's neither here nor there. But Rachel Herrenrath made our lives so wretched toward the last that the gentry abovestairs found she'd have to go, not in the fortnight she was given, but overnight. And so she did. And no tears from us, as you may believe."

I did not resent the pride with which she avoided my accusation, I was ever one to admire pride, more especially in the lower orders, for I felt it a necessary adjunct to men and women in positions of service, as was my own condition. But Mrs. Kempson had not precisely answered my question, and I wondered if this was deliberate.

"Forgive me, Mrs. Kempson, but I have been puzzled by one thing. This woman departed in haste, as you say, but this was several weeks ago. I found what appeared to be the rest of her entire possessions in her apartments abovestairs."

"I daresay she will come for them one bad day," the cook remarked, slapping the dough she had rolled and kneading it a second time. "But she'd best take none of her airs about me."

To placate her, I said, "I'm sure she will not annoy you, Mrs. Kempson. I'm afraid it is I she will resent."

I was relieved to see that she appeared mollified, and I did not at all mind her slightly sinister warning, "Pay her no mind, miss. No mind at all as to her manners. Be on your guard though, for she's not one to take a successor to her bosom. She'd as soon murder you as say 'good day.' But you'll soon be getting the better of her, I am persuaded."

On that warning note, I went on to choose a chambermaid and under footman and sent them to the dusty apartments on the top floor with orders to remove all small items. As for the rest, I asked the grumbling old coachman to send up the strongest pair of stablehands, and I returned to my room to change into my oldest gown, a shabby, faded green worsted, one of those disreputable costumes ideally suited to battling cobwebs and the dust of a score of years.

While we were hard at work with everything in the middle of the floor, I was abruptly summoned to Miss Amanda's apartment. It was just before noon, and her bed-sitting room might have been sunny and comfortable but for her obviously depressed state, which caused her to leave the portieres drawn, the room in a dreary blue dusk, and herself in an unflattering mustard brown dress. The color and poor style of the gown only emphasized what I was sure was her deep grief at her grandfather's death. She stood at the door, looking so old I might have supposed she was her own mother.

"Come in. You are not dressed very properly for the burial, Miss Killain."

When I had come into the room, I said softly, "No, miss. I beg your pardon, but I was not asked to appear. Mrs. Dalreagh has said nothing to me since Dr. Malcolm was here this morning."

She had been weeping, and her eyes were swollen and red. I felt great sympathy for the girl, but she was not the sort who would accept casually expressed sympathy.

"I don't doubt it. That creature knows a great deal more about Grandpapa's murder than she will say. Why else do you think she requires laudanum before she can close her eyes of nights?"

Startled, I could only echo, "Murder? Surely, miss, that is going it rather too strong!"

"Not strong enough." She had been folding satin and superfine garments, of a last century cut, trying to collect all of her grandfather's things; she stopped now, her fingers shaking.

When she looked at me, I was appalled by the hatred in her eyes. "It was you who murdered him, at my precious stepmother's order. The question is, how did you contrive it? I have puzzled over that all day. It is the only thing that keeps me from running mad at the horrors I have seen in this house."

I do not recall when I have felt so miserable, so guilty.

"Miss Amanda! You cannot believe this dreadful thing. I left him only a few minutes. I went to put away the— Oh, all that is of no account now. But you must believe I liked the small gentleman. I do not even know what killed him, what he saw . . ."

She wiped her eyes with a heavy cambric handkerchief, afterward studying me as I spoke. Her expression made me feel that she debated not my crime but the method of its commission.

"I knew when she was permitted to send for you that you would be one of her hirelings. Rachel feared it would be so. She warned me. Now, where is Rachel?"

I discovered, rather vaguely, for I had been too busy to think of it, that I had the beginnings of a dreadful headache. But as I put my hand up, with an unthinking gesture, still staring at her in disbelief, her heavy features seemed to grow larger, closer. She peered into my face near-sightedly. Surprised at my own reaction, I found myself physically afraid of her. I managed to stand my ground without retreating, but I confess the instinct was there.

"I know nothing of Mrs. Herrenrath," I said in the calmest voice I could muster. "I only know that she must be expecting to return, for the storage chamber is filled with her boxes and trunks, and Monsieur Minotte informed us only yesterday that she calls for various articles now and again."

I knew the instant I mentioned the tutor's name that the overwrought girl had begun to have doubts about her accusation. However, though she avoided my eyes and went on with her sad work, she threw out one more bitter accusation, as if unable to let me leave her in any kind of peace.

"Well, run about your busy day, Miss Killain. I daresay you have many other little tasks to perform for Lucie . . . that is to say, the Honorable Mrs. Dalreagh."

My Irish temper smoldered and threatened to burst into flame, but I have faced such crises before and managed to overcome the desire to shout, to scream like a fishwife, and to strike back with the truth.

"Yes, miss," I bobbed to a quick curtsy. "Thank you, miss." Another curtsy. "If I may go now."

"Yes, yes. Certainly." She waved me away exactly as I had often been waved away twelve years before, when I was a scullery maid. It was lowering, both to my spirits and to my position; but there are worse disasters in the world, and I left the apartment of the unhappy young woman.

I think it was my understanding that she was so bitterly unhappy which made it possible for me to recover my usual calm by the time I reached the dusty, cobwebbed rooms where the cleaning went on at a fine rate. The recent repression of my emotions proved, as always, a signal for much pounding, shaking, and cleaning. It was an excellent antidote to the poisonous atmosphere among the women of Mist House.

After I had dismissed everyone and sent them all off to take a luncheon, I found it relieved my mind of Miss Amanda's recent accusations when I set about replacing all the furniture as best I could, and a reasonably pleasant set of guest chambers resulted only just in time.

The gentry had begun to arrive for the burying of Sir Peveril before I was notified, but I was relieved to know that there were rooms properly aired and prepared for each of them.

The maid, Phoebe, brought warm water and napkins for me to wash off the dirt of the cleaning hours, and then she lingered for a bit of gossip.

"Young madam's awake, but only just.

Would you believe it, mum, she'd so little care for Sir Peveril's murder that she took her usual powders and went off to sleep as innocent as a babe."

"Whatever do you mean, Sir Peveril's murder?" I repeated a little more sharply than I would have done had I not been shaken by my recent encounter with Amanda Dalreagh.

"But it's talked of among the staff, ma'am, that there's been some oddities about and that the new housekeeper would change all. She's a gift for it, they do say. Is it true, ma'am?"

"I don't know," I replied in confusion. "However, I shall expect the truth reported to me, and if it is, I shall not be angry, no matter what the provocation. You do understand me, Phoebe?"

"I think so, mum," she replied in what I could only interpret, reluctantly, as the utmost indifference to the seriousness of the situation here at Mist House. "I'll be most happy to give any little help you desire, mum. Though I'll be fair to warn you, you've but said to me the very same words as Old Herring." She stopped, gasped, and murmured with an irritating giggle, "And who's to say when we'll be seeing Old Herring again. Bad luck she was. And run for her very life. She's not like to be coming back in broad light of day."

"Thank you, Phoebe," I said briskly, feeling

all the shame of listening to such obvious gossip.

The girl finally accepted the hint and went about her work, leaving me to recall her words in connection with the warning hint of Mrs. Kempson earlier in the day. Then I regretted my own stupidity in not pursuing the talk of Sir Peveril's supposed murder much further, for servants have a way of getting secret information much more swiftly than do the gentry. But it was too late now, at least for the moment.

I changed my garments and put on my best black gown, a dress I wore only for solemn occasions, as it invariably drew color from me and gave me an exceedingly somber look, which matched my mood at this time. While I dressed, there was some commotion on the moat bridge far below my window. I went over and looked down. The stableman had come out to greet who I supposed must be the first guest for the funeral—but it was the Earl of Dalreagh, who rode up to be greeted by the House servants with an enthusiasm I could not mistake. To my surprise, his manservant, Hobbs, sat his own mount tolerably well and came trooping along behind Richard Dalreagh, only to be likewise smothered in the chatter by those of the household who wished to be first to tell bad news.

I turned away from the window, conscious of

two things: first, that His Lordship would be excessively disappointed and perhaps deeply moved over the disasters that had occurred in his absence; and second, that he might have occasion to consult me now and again on the running of the household. I expected no more and would be grateful for the moments of business that brought us together. Nevertheless, I was profoundly troubled over our first meeting since the death of Sir Peveril Wye; for he might well share the feelings of his niece, and even perhaps of Mrs. Kempson, that I had been criminally remiss there.

I waited until I was sure all the members of the household as well as the guests were in the burial ground outside Mist House before I went out as unobtrusively as possible to stand with Mrs. Kempson in our special place behind the gentry and just before the household servants. I have always found it difficult to place myself precisely during such formal moments; for a great deal depends on my employers, some of whom regard me as a kind of upper servant, while others, like Miss Hunnicut and my recent Irish employers, placed me on a level of pseudo-gentility with governesses, tutors, and the local apothecary and surgeon. It was obvious to me today as Mrs. Kempson and I watched the somber proceedings of the service and burial under the crisp, bright sky that at Mist House I would do well to remember "my place" at all times. There were a number of guests, from neighboring great houses and the village, no doubt, but having prepared their bedchambers and seen to the menu for the night and morrow, I had no more to do with them unless summoned; and none of the ladies and gentlemen glanced at me.

This was quite as satisfactory to me. It gave me a chance to study the burial ground itself. It must have been started centuries before, to judge by the age of the gravestones, possibly even when the Abbey was taken over by the Dalreagh family at the time of the closing of the religious houses under Henry the Eighth. There were certain distinctive marks of the burials of many Dalreaghs, more particularly wherever the earth was sunken in a coffin shape, a depressing fact that I found true of all graveyards. None of the stones, however, gave me the cold shivers I felt in the crypt.

Miss Amanda, stony-faced and red-eyed, ignored me. She stood at the right of her uncle, the Earl, while Lucie Dalreagh was at his left, fragile, silently weeping, looking for all the world as if she had dearly loved the father of her predecessor. I would have been more touched by her excess of emotion had I not seen her the previous night, so very concerned with other mysterious matters, of which the tutor had some awareness. I confess, though, that whatever direction my troubled thoughts took, they returned inevitably to the tall form of Richard Dalreagh. I felt sure that with his capable presence we should have a quieter night ahead—which only proves that I am not gifted as a prophet.

It was curious about Lucie Dalreagh, though. As the vicar of the local church completed his few but excellently chosen words in praise of Sir Peveril, who had, quite obviously, been a particular favorite of the district, and I heard the deep, hollow, poignant sounds of earth piled upon the coffin, I caught a side-glance exchanged between Lucie and the Frenchman. In her expressive face was such terror as arrested all my accusatory thoughts toward her. The Earl looked at her and then at Louis Minotte farther away along the head of the grave. His Lordship frowned at what I suppose he thought was indiscreet behavior and in bad taste, for he was placed so that he could see only the exchange of glances, not the terror in Lucie's eyes. Perhaps, he was moved by the attitude of the other guests, who fidgeted and occasionally whispered to each other in a way the Earl probably found significant.

Lucie's thin, lacy handkerchief was now sodden, and she groped for another in her reticule, but failing to find it, looked to Monsieur Minotte. He started to reach for his own larger and more competent handkerchief when he intercepted a look from Richard Dalreagh that froze him in mid-gesture. After that, Lucie sniffed vainly and irritatingly during the interment, until the Earl, out of all patience, handed her his own handkerchief and bade her, in the most frigid tones, to "stop sniffing." Were the moment less serious, I should have been inclined to smile at her chastisement; she behaved so exactly like a child, ill-taught in manners, who is being publicly scolded.

Presently, the family left the graveside, the Earl taking a hard grip on Lucie's delicate wrist and all but rushing her ahead of him toward the great, gray pile of stones that was Mist House. They were closely followed by Monsieur Minotte, looking even more somber than usual in his customary black, but I was relieved to see that he politely offered his arm to Amanda, who blushed and accepted—but with one last look at the coffin now covered by the earth.

Mrs. Kempson muttered to me, " 'Twas the ghostly Abbess, you know. That'll be how the wee gentleman died. We know now that the creature exists."

I looked at her, questioning not her statement that the Abbess had killed Sir Peveril by frightening him, but her assumption that the Abbess was a ghost and not flesh and blood.

"Can it be someone in the household?" I asked, half to myself and half for her opinion. She could not help knowing the household better than I.

"That'll not be for the likes of us to say, miss. But it's my opinion—only a thought, mind—that there *is* such creatures as phantasms, and we've got ourselves one of 'em here at Mist House. And what's more," she stared hard at me, "I'll make you a wager she rests by daylight among them statutes in the crypt. What d'you think on that, now?"

I felt chilled to the bone, but whether from the brisk and windy day or the thought of that crypt as a resting place for ghosts I was not prepared to say. I stood there staring at the sexton and his muscular assistant as they completed their task, and presently, I realized that Mrs. Kempson and the servants had returned to the house.

As for me, I felt impelled to remain out of doors under the bright afternoon sky of winter while I assembled my thoughts about the unfortunate little man whose coffin was now hidden from sight. I attempted to recall precisely his last words to me. Perhaps, there would be in them some clue that I had not heretofore understood.

I stepped around the grave and found myself on a well-trodden path that led in a westerly direction toward the distant purple hills called The Peaks. It was a comfort to be alone for these few minutes, away from servants, cooks, weeping women, embittered women, and talk of that ghostly apparition that had, the night before, possibly accounted for another victim.

I felt the brisk rush of the wind curling against my cheek, the sun in my eyes, and I wondered what strange creature had cursed Mist House with its presence. If the guilty thing was human, some person I had met, I could not imagine which of the inhabitants of the ancient building might have reached out its hand to Sir Peveril, dealing death in the chapel.

By one of those coincidences that fill me with dread, suddenly a hand touched my shoulder. I knew not whether to scream or run.

10

"Now, what the devil will you be wanting of me?" I demanded as I turned aggressively to hide my fears.

"Only your company and the answers to a few questions, in that order," said His Lordship, Richard Dalreagh. He smiled in the way which had moved me almost from the first moment of our meeting, but I was well aware of the stern, contemptuous manner he had used toward Lucie was still present behind the charming, if imperious facade that I admired so much.

I stopped in midstep because I could scarcely do anything else. Richard Dalreagh's strength, at least the strength of his arm, was prodigious. When he saw me glance sardonically at his hand, he dropped his arm and stepped up beside me.

"I have you to thank, I believe, that I was enabled to return to the house, though only just in time for the burial. Is it true, Anne? Was it you who gave the leggy boy his instructions?"

I was not at all sure his manner was as pleasant as it seemed, and I answered with great care.

"There seemed to be no effort made to handle the matter of Sir Peveril's death, so I sent the boy, Your Lordship. But I was given a severe scold for it. Mrs. Dalreagh felt I had exceeded my authority. As indeed, I did," I answered truthfully.

As I had suspected, he was not really interested in that but in various other aspects of the dreadful business. We walked on up the path between rolling greenery which seemed to be still standing in water from the storm two days previous. I felt a surprising companionable quality in him, surprising because of his title and his great estate, which were all-important in Georgian England.

"That's of no consequence. But I am puzzled by my sister-in-law's other accusations. Are you aware of them?"

I considered a moment, screening my eyes from the late sunlight.

"I daresay she believes I should have prevented the small gentleman's death."

Had he leaped to the same assumption, I should have risen in all my Irish fury to demand justice and insist that I could have acted in no other way, but I saw his quick scowl of impatience and guessed even before he spoke that he would dismiss her charge as absurd.

"What rubbish is this? Does she think you

should have stood up to some assassin in the dark? How could you have prevented Wye's death? He had a bad heart. He was an old man." Lord Richard glanced back. We had been mounting rapidly, and the Dalreagh graveyard lay almost directly below us. The great, empty grave, so large for the little man, was now filled, but the blackness of the soil made the shape of the grave stand out fresh and clear against the grass-covered burial ground and all the scattered stones that marked the previous burials. Lord Richard said softly, "I liked him, the little man. I once rather hoped he would be my own father." He shrugged, smiled. "But it was not to be. For some incomprehensible reason, his daughter chose to marry my brother, Kevin."

I said suddenly, on the spur of the moment, "Miss Amanda might have been Your Lordship's daughter."

He gave me an odd look. "Why do you say that, Anne? Has she given you any difficulty? She *is* a strange girl. I cannot begin to understand her."

"Perhaps it is her unhappiness that baffles you, my Lord."

"Does she seem unhappy to you? Perhaps you can tell me why."

I thought I detected a note of veiled resentment here, as though I had charged him with his niece's unhappiness.

"I should imagine her unhappiness is due to—" I was nearly guilty of an indiscretion here that might have had monstrous waves of repercussion, involving as it did a woman presumably still in mourning for her recently dead husband. And of course, there was another reason for holding my tongue: The matter was not my concern. I hastily changed my words. "—due to the death of her father so recently and now of her grandfather."

"Very true." He looked down at me in a special way, both tender and a little sad, which made me feel warm with the desire to possess his good opinion. "You are a wise girl, I think, Anne. Wise and discreet."

"Thank you, sir." We had paused to look back over the burial ground, and when we started on, he took my arm, and we climbed together past one of the low stone walls that cut across many of the hillsides. I said presently, "You have not yet asked how Sir Peveril died, and yet, I am quite sure it is the first question you wished to charge me with."

He said nothing for a moment. I wondered if he would lie to me. He did not, and I was immensely relieved.

"Yes. I should like to know, from your lips, what really happened last night. I feel reasonably sure—in any case, I hope—it will be more intelligent than the tale they have been telling me at the house."

I smiled faintly. "I'm very much afraid Your Lordship will find my tale just as preposterous as whatever the ladies have told you. Sir Peveril died in my arms, crying out his fear of the Black Abbess."

I told him the full circumstances, how I found the little man huddled in the doorway of the crypt, muttering that he had seen the Abbess, how I brought him to the chapel to await me, and then, minutes later, the terrible scream.

"The fault was mine. I should never have left him. He had already warned me that he was frightened of something . . . of some one. My Lord!" I turned to him earnestly. "There *is* something frightful in that house. Literally frightful."

His expression changed in a subtle way. It did not make him less handsome. It only made him less attractive, because he appeared to believe me no longer. He said coolly, "I trust you are not about to join that idiotic crew that prates about nuns, abbesses, and other spirit visitors. I did not really believe you capable of such talk."

"I am perfectly capable of it, Your Lordship." My voice was as crisp and cold as his, even to my own ears. I felt hurt and disappointed in him for his unreasonable attitude. Surely, he must know I would not be given to wild fancies if there were any possible alternative. I added before he could go on with his comments, "I really must return to the house. There is much to be done and the apartments of the funeral guests to see to."

"Yes. Of course. I had forgotten for the moment."

I turned and then looked down, significantly, waiting for him to remove his hand from my arm. For a minute, it did not appear that he would. He stood there, looking at my arm and his hand so strangely that I did not know what to say or do. I remained still until he said, "Go back to the arrogant females you serve, but if you run on any more abbesses or floating ghostly nuns, come to *me,* and we will seek them out together."

I smiled, secretly much relieved, but retaining that reserve which I felt due to my position and his. Then, I agreed that I would do so, and he raised his hand. I was free and hurried back down the hill toward the burial ground. I could still feel the warmth on my arm where each of his fingers had caught and held me. When I looked back, he had gone on. I wondered how I could care for the opinion, and the glance and touch, of a man I scarcely knew, a supercilious, haughty peer of England who, for all his pretended attentions to me, never forgot that I was one of those tiresome "idiotic" servants.

Exceedingly thoughtful, I went about my duties during the rest of the day. A number of the guests called on my assistance in obtaining various little items needed to make their stay "a pleasant and memorable one," as a lady from Lincoln informed me. I soon discovered that this was the attitude of most of the guests. Scarcely any of them had come to pay their last respects to Sir Peveril. It was not too difficult to understand what seemed, on the surface, to be their cruel indifference. There are few occasions for meetings, visits, and public gatherings in that part of the country during the depth of winter. It was a human reaction; I have encountered it before. I busied myself as much as possible so that I might avoid uncomfortable thoughts.

I ate a very late supper in my own sitting room long after the dinner served in the Great Hall for the guests and hosts of Mist House. Though it was long after dark, with the candelabra lighted in both rooms of the apartment, I left open the portieres of the sitting room windows and ate a slice of roasted fowl, embellished with turnips and potatoes in Mrs. Kempson's special sauce, and the whole followed by an omelette filled with the spiced jelly made from berries gathered on the estate. The whole of the meal was delicious enough to restore my good feeling about the world. During my meal, I enjoyed the view of the early night from my windows. The sky was swept clear and piercingly blue, and later came the deep blue of night, a cold night of stars.

The wind that had felt so exhilarating after the depressing moments at the graveside, now whirled about the ancient house, roaring, and, a few minutes later, moaning pitifully around the corners of the Abbey portion of Mist House. Such a rackety sound the wind made that I did not at once hear the knocking on the door. When the wind slackened briefly, I heard the sound, wondered who wished my help at this hour, and hoped it was not a critical matter. I was tired, and I was thinking about a night's uninterrupted sleep until I opened the sitting room door.

Richard Dalreagh stood there, imposing, even forbidding, yet obviously making an effort to be congenial.

"Forgive me. I know I interrupt you."

"No, no," I said hastily, hoping my hair and gown looked neat and that I did not appear too eager. "What is it Your Lordship wishes?"

His mouth twisted with what I thought of as a whimsical impatience. I was aware, as I had been once or twice before, of a sensuous quality which gave warmth to a splendid face that might otherwise be coldly arrogant.

"Anne, must you always give me my full title? It occupies so damnably much time." When I was too dumbfounded to reply to this, he went on, briskly efficient, very much the Earl of Dalreagh. "In any case, that is not what I came to discuss with you."

"No, my Lord," I replied, barely concealing a smile. "Nor did I suppose so. How may I assist you?"

"Come along."

"Certainly, my Lord. Where to?"

I did not look in the least surprised but stepped out into the corridor before him and closed my door. He appeared a trifle dazed, muttered something about my disgusting efficiency, and motioned me to follow him. I supposed there was something amiss in the bedchambers of the guests, but instead, we stopped at the gallery door and went down the stone steps toward the chapel below. I possessed no tender memories of this spot and dreaded entering the damp, depressing place where I had found Sir Peveril crawling with his dying strength in an attempt to escape the thing that terrorized him. I could not help feeling, despite my company, that whatever had frightened the old gentleman might still *be* somewhere within this ancient, ghost-ridden place.

It was perfectly obvious, however, that Richard Dalreagh had no such fears. Dressed as he was for dinner, and, I confess, looking splendid to my eyes in his fashionable dark pantaloons and coat, with the snowy folds of his scarf for contrast, he might have appeared absurd among the cobwebs of the Abbey. From the way he strode in and looked around, staring hard at the place before the altar where Sir Peveril died, I suspected he would be perfectly at home in any setting, except, perhaps, a very humble one.

"So this is where he saw our busy 'Abbess'! Did he give you no other clue?"

"None. It was most strange. I left him so short a time, and I am sure there was no one in the place before the altar where Sir Peveril low."

He walked around the entire chapel and through the cloister, asking me if it was possible I could have missed anyone hidden in the shadow of the cloister, which suggested to me that he suspected Sir Peveril's death was contrived by someone present in Mist House. When I explained that I had looked into those shadows, he stared at me, shaking his head. But he said nothing of his thoughts and returned to me. We walked out to the steps of the crypt.

"Now then, when you left Wye, you took those steps and stored some garments in the chamber beside the crypt. Is that so?"

"Quite, my Lord. I was carrying a very full armload of Mrs. Herrenrath's property, and I had been told that her other boxes, cases, and portmanteaus were in that chamber."

He did not seem too interested in the matter of the recent housekeeper but asked casually as we went down the steps, "And did you find some of her bandboxes in the chamber?"

"I found nothing else." The discovery seemed so odd at the time, but no one since had been in the least surprised. Now, when I repeated the story to the Earl as we approached the little chamber, I became aware once more of something very strange about that chamber being filled with what should have been the entire possessions of Rachel Herrenrath.

"No other storage items?" he asked, showing his first interest in the subject. "But that closet is rather large, as I recall. If it was filled with Rachel Herrenrath's property, there must be a deal of it present."

"A great amount. So much so that I cannot help wondering why she has not sent for it."

"Well, well, we'll see. Give me your keys." He set his lamp in my hand, took the keys off my belt, and tried three in the lock. I pointed out the correct key, and the door swung open. In the second or two it took for the door to open, I had a sort of chilling fear that I would find something deadly within the crowded closet. The Earl pushed the door open far enough so that I could see into the chamber. Nothing appeared as I expected, nothing at all, not the deadly Thing I half-feared and not Mrs. Herrenrath's luggage crowding the room. Nothing but a soiled bandbox and the bundle of used clothing I had brought down last night.

"But it's all wrong!" I cried, momentarily panicked by something that seemed impossible. "The chamber was full of her things last night. Where can they have gone?"

The Earl looked into the room and around, even at the ceiling. He shrugged.

"They are certainly not here, now."

Affronted, I said sharply, "Do you think I am a liar, sir?"

He seemed torn between impatience and laughter.

"Good God, no! Don't be so prickly, Anne. There are still some of her things here. It is a very dark chamber. Perhaps you saw—"

"I know what I saw, my Lord. The Chamber was full of her things, and now they are gone. That much my eyes tell me."

He stepped back out of the chamber, locked the door, and gave me the keys, which I accepted with stiff, cold fingers. I was both angry and confused by the disappearance of Rachel Herrenrath's property. Had I not considered my word challenged by His Lordship, I should have come to some logical explanation about that nearly empty storage chamber. In the circumstances, I simply could not collect my wits at that precise minute when I needed them.

He looked into my face and took my chin between his thumb and forefinger.

"I do believe you, you know. Why should you be so concerned about that woman's property? In all likelihood, she has sent for it, and it was delivered to her. You see? Quite simple."

"Where?" I asked him, point-blank.

"What do you mean, where?"

"Where to? Where *is* Rachel Herrenrath? Where were her things delivered?"

"A thousand places. She could be anywhere. I will certainly find out, if it means so much to you to know. But I warn you, you won't be too fond of the lady when you meet. She was an aggressive creature at best, and a bit of a prowling, prying old—woman. I had complaints from everyone." He thought a moment and added in a voice of surprise, "All except Amanda. I wonder why." He shrugged, apparently considered my foolish question, and before I could divine his intention, he kissed me, lightly, almost playfully, on the lips. I was too astonished either to resist or to reply in the same way. He looked at me rather a long time, said gently, "Forgive me, Anne Killain, but it was very tempting," and moved away from me a few steps toward the archway of the crypt. He glanced into the big, vaulted chamber, frowning, broke a cobweb at one side of the arch, and motioned me to join him as he raised the lamp, the better to see the solemn, echoing place.

"Ghastly notion, living above the dead," he said harshly. "I used to be terrified of this place when I was a child."

When I moved up behind him, I saw again that curious, almost geometric aspect of the ancient crypt. There were long, attenuated shadows wherever statues marked the burial places of the ancient Abbey's inhabitants.

"The Abbey must have had great wealth," I observed, considering the strange stone creatures flickering in the lamplight all around us.

He looked at the gray tombs which appeared to be marble but in some cases were not, as he informed me with a smile. "Scarcely the half of them are marble. A few abbesses and one stray bishop who succumbed while visiting the Abbey." He used the lamp to point out a tomb at the far end of the hall, and I exclaimed in some amusement, "No. Please! When you do that the lamp flickers, and I have a horrid notion that all these stone creatures are alive."

"And," he went on quickly, "the statues are not all stone. At least half of them—these two, for example—are of clay. So you see, our historic and religious charmers were mere mortals, after all."

I was astonished at this disclosure and was fingering the somber figure that loomed above me when His Lordship added, "You will find the same is true of our famed Black Abbess."

I laughed. "How disillusioning!"

When I looked away from the clay nun, I found the Earl's eyes on me and could not mistake his interest in me. I felt my cheeks flush as though I were a child of twelve and was profoundly relieved when he looked away. But then he startled me by remarking suddenly, "What the devil *is* in here with us?"

11

I swung around, almost expecting to see that shrouded creature, the Black Abbess, looming up over us in the arched entrance to the crypt. Nothing was there but darkness. I saw that His Lordship was raising the lamp to illuminate the far corner of the vaulted room, and I stood on tiptoe, trying to discover what it was that disturbed the Earl. He said severely, "Come out. You are no longer hidden, you know."

I waited to see if his peremptory command would be answered, much less obeyed. I was sure that the darkness as well as the number of statues and coffins that separated us from the far end of the hall also concealed the hidden creature. However, his gamble paid off. We both saw someone rise from a coffin behind one of the statues at the same time that a metal weapon fell to the stone floor with resounding metallic clang.

"So, it's you, Amanda," my companion called out. "What new statues have you been slapping together?"

"I did not intend to eavesdrop, Uncle," said the girl, picking up some sort of small, flat knife and then dropping it again as she came around into our view. Her black mourning gown was speckled with odd gray spots which I presently realized were clay.

"Come here and join us, Amanda. Show us what you have accomplished down here." He glanced at me, explaining with a wry little smile. "A morbid taste, but undeniably a talent. My niece found a number of the statues had fallen to pieces, and she has constructed some rather exceptional replacements." He guessed my surprise and reminded me, "I told you many of them were clay."

So many strange things had occurred at Mist House during the past month since Kevin Dalreagh's death that I wondered at Miss Amanda's courage in working down here at night among these shadowy images of the dead. While I was wondering at this strange occupation, Lord Richard set down the lamp and began to brush the girl off, while asking her with amused impatience, "How do you see to work in the dark? Are you fond of ghosts? Have a care, or you may find yourself doing the Black Abbess in clay . . ." He lowered his hand and gestured for me to complete his work. "Miss Killain, see if you can make my niece presentable."

As lightly as possible, I tried to resume

brushing her off, but she drew away from me as though mine was a demon's touch. She plainly cared about her uncle's good opinion, however.

"I had a candle with a reflector. It was perfectly good for my work, and I thought, after Grandpapa's burying, that the work would take my mind off—things."

"I know, Amanda. It has been very hard for you." The tenderness in his voice touched me. I suspected that despite his hauteur and his sardonic way, he cared very deeply for the family that was only indirectly his responsibility. "So, you snuffed the candle and worked in the dark, as I've heard some stone-carving geniuses do." He was smiling, but she refused to be drawn to see any humor in the moment.

"No. I became tired, and I went off to sleep. The candle burned down. Papa always warned me not to work here without a long wick. Papa always—" She began to cry, not daintily, like her stepmother, but harshly and deeply, and when the Earl put his arm around her, pulling her to him, she seemed to gain comfort. He looked over her head at me.

"I had best take her to her room. Would you be good enough to gather up her materials? The crypt is sometimes damp when the river rises, and her instruments will rust."

"Of course, sir. At once."

He gave me the lamp, and he led the girl to the dark archway while I moved toward the far end of the crypt with the light. Even safe in the comfortable knowledge that Richard Dalreagh stood at the door of the crypt, I was oppressed by the great, looming figures as I passed them one by one. I had resolved not to look at those gray sentinels, but in spite of all my intentions, I found myself staring uneasily upward, only to see again the gray faces outlined by their coifs, the empty eye-sockets seeming to return my gaze, impassive as death.

Beneath the long wooden block lying across a coffin was an assortment of colored clays and the beginnings of a molded head which, I thought, showed considerable talent. It slightly resembled Amanda but was thinner, more fragile. I suspected it was her dead mother whose head she was doing from painful and loving memory. Amanda's tools shone on the smooth stone floor at the back wall, where traces of river water had seeped in, collecting among tiny pools in the long-eroded stone. I took up the odd instruments, a flat-bladed knife, a sharp instrument, very thin, with one end clawed, and several others, including one blade of a pair of shears. I took them up in a dirty rag and brought them with me. We all went up the stone steps, and I bade the two of them good night as I went into my own sitting room.

His Lordship looked back at me, smiled, and then he and the girl seemed to melt into the dusty, candlelit distance of the Long Gallery.

We had all been so busy with our separate and troublesome thoughts that I found Miss Amanda's tools still in my hand when I was closing the door. I stepped out in the corridor to return the tools, but both the Earl and his niece were gone from my sight, and the Long Gallery lay before me, shimmering in moonlight that filtered through from the windows above the interior courtyard. Some chambermaid had left several windows partially open, but there seemed to be no harm done, I supposed, and the Gallery would be the better for some fresh air.

I went to bed shortly after, having bathed very hastily and used towels with almost brutal roughness, for the water in the hip bath delivered by one of the footmen during my absence in the crypt had turned chill in the meantime.

Whether it was the brisk toweling or simply the result of a long day, I went off to sleep almost immediately and did not awaken until the moon was down, a little after two in the morning, at which time I became gradually aware of a dull headache brought about by a pounding or slamming sound somewhere not far away. My windows had both come unfastened, I thought, and were banging in the wind.

Still half asleep, I rose, took up my robe, and wandered across the bedchamber to examine the window latch. It seemed secure. Outside lay the enormous night, with the stars still out in frozen little gleams of light. But beyond, to the south and west, where the raw peaks seemed to make a long rent in the sky, I saw clouds crossing over into our pleasant, cold night, driven by the wind. I looked down at that relatively modern eighteenth-century replacement for the ancient moat bridge and saw that the water in the river beneath had risen during the last few hours. Yes. There was a storm somewhere, no doubt high among the Peaks.

Then, I thought of the dampness from the moat seeping in among those stone coffins and those strange and terrible images of the dead. The thought made me pull in the windows and latch them again securely. Now that I was on my feet and sufficiently awakened, I went into the sitting room and tried the window there. It too was safely latched. I knew now, however, where the banging windows or shutters came from. They were undoubtedly the windows in the Long Gallery that overlooked the inner courtyard. With the wind and the rising storm, this noise could only increase, perhaps doing damage both to the windows and the courtyard below.

In no pleasant temper at this, the total destruction of my night's sleep, I went back, stepped into my night slippers, and then, being too impatient for any nervous qualms, I unbolted the door to the chapel steps, crossed the landing, and entered the Long Gallery. It was freezing cold and lighted faintly by the stairs. Having woken up in the dark and become used to it during the past few minutes, I needed no candle, whose light would doubtless blow out at once anyway in the drafty long hall. I hurried along to the first open window and reaching out over the courtyard, pulled it in very hard, in fact, slamming it shut. The courtyard, far below, looked gloomy and cold, arousing in me the opposite emotion from that which I had felt the morning before, when it looked so sunny and inviting.

I repeated the noisy act of closing the other windows until I reached the end of the gallery, where I looked into the corridor beyond. This led past the newly refurbished bedchambers where the guests were, or should have been, sleeping at the moment. Everything seemed serene and quiet. Only the night wind moaned around corners and swept toward me, whipping at my garments, lashing my hair across my face.

I stepped back around the corner into the Long Gallery and started toward my own rooms. There was still a noticeable draft, though the windows were closed. I made out the open embrasures or peepholes in the wall to my left and remembered that they looked down on the Great Hall three stories below. Very probably, they explained the drafts. I stopped before the first embrasure and held up my hand. The air felt fetid and yet bitter cold against my palm. My curiosity got the better of my impatience to return to bed. I looked through the peephole and saw exactly what I had expected to see, which is to say, nothing but the huge interior lighted dimly by one wall sconce on the chapel wall at the far end.

Somewhere in the Great Hall there were doors open to create such a draft. I moved to the next embrasure but still could not get a clear view of each sector of the hall. In any case, I had no intention of going down there to see to any open doors, no matter how great the draft. I was much too sleepy, too tired, and, perhaps, too cowardly to go. But I was also curious and puzzled.

At the third embrasure, I discovered that the two north doors nearest the breakfast parlor were open wide. Behind these open doors and across the hall was the regularly used staircase from the upper stories. Obviously, the draft came from there. I wondered if the doors had stood open all evening. I thought it unlikely; for if they had been, Lord Richard would have felt it as he took his niece along the gallery to her bedchamber, and I doubted that he would have retired without bolting the doors to prevent the further draft and the noise of the wind.

At the last embrasure, I discovered who had opened those two doors. Lucie Dalreagh moved slowly across the hall toward the chapel door. She was obviously walking in her sleep at an odd, faltering pace, her white, filmy garments floating behind her, her bare feet pale in the faint light. Something about the look of her seemed more strange than all the rest. And then I remembered. The draft should have blown her garments forward, not pressed them against her thin, slight form until she very much resembled one of those beautiful carved female figures one sees below the bowsprit of a sailing vessel.

I stood on tiptoe and called to her. It was a long way down, and I knew there was a chance my disembodied voice might terrify her, even if she was awakened by it. Nevertheless, I put all my authority into the call and saw her pause and turn and look all around. It must have been an eery experience for her, and I wondered what thoughts must be filling her brain now, since she still seemed asleep, though I was fairly sure her large, vacant blue eyes were open.

I gave up the attempt to wake her. I had, after all, interfered with Sir Peveril's night prowling, and he was dead. It was certainly not in my duties to risk Lucie's life as well. She had doubtless been walking in her sleep for weeks, perhaps even years, and no harm ever came to her.

I continued my walk through the Long Gallery, wondering which of two destinations Lucie's strange, somnambulistic state demanded of her. She was either bound for the chapel and perhaps the crypt or she intended to mount the chapel steps that led past my bedchamber and out into the Long Gallery. Having failed to rouse her, I was not at all sure I wanted to encounter her in that gloomy corridor.

I was not even sure she was walking in her sleep. It occurred to me, among other chilling possibilities, that the sweet, stupid Lucie Fairburn who invariably got her way in those far-off school days might very possibly have learned how useful her old tricks could be when there were larger stakes.

Could it be the ghostly, floating Lucie that the unfortunate Sir Peveril saw and mistook for the Abbess? And there was unquestionably a suspicion of her which Dr. Malcolm had expressed when he mentioned that her husband died so painfully. There were many things, among them the complaints Lucie made about Rachel Herrenrath's "spying," a natural reaction for a woman with deadly secrets to conceal. The "why" of her conduct seemed more obvious. There was probably considerable money or property involved. Something of that sort, at least. Perhaps in Sir Peveril's death she profited materially. I did not know how. That was no more in my province than this spying on her now.

I shivered over the notion of her possible guilt, however, reflecting that it would not be the first time I had discovered the monster beneath the "helpless innocent" surface. I hurried along the gallery toward my rooms, making the resolve to discuss this problem with His Lordship and let him decide what was the best way of countering not only Lucie's somnambulism but my suspicions of its cause and its deadly effect.

I heard then an iron-bound door slam shut, the sound rushing up the chapel steps and into the Long Gallery between me and the safety of my rooms. I stopped nervously, was angered at my own cowardice, and stepped forward. I did not quite have the courage to go across those wretched chapel steps and into my bedchamber. Instead, I walked a few steps farther, along the front corridor and into my sitting room.

It was as dark as I had left it, but the odor of something new and strange was in the room. Or in the adjoining bedchamber. I could not remember what it put me in mind of, except that all things strange and foreign were suspect to me now. I reached out in the dark, found a candlestick under my groping fingers, and took it up as a possible weapon. I walked carefully into the bedchamber—and saw my visitor, that white and drifting creature, standing in the open doorway that led to the chapel steps. I understood the now hauntingly familiar scent which had puzzled and warned me when I entered. It was a particular perfume I never used, subtle but pervasive.

12

Lucie Dalreagh, for some reason which did not reassure me, had decided to visit me in the dark. It was not the friendliest meeting, and I wished very much that I knew for a certainty what her business with me really was and why she had been so determined on my coming to Mist House, when she obviously had very little regard for me.

My heart was thundering in my bosom at this eery sight in the darkness, but I managed to say quietly, with some effort at my usual composure, "It is quite late, madam. Are you well? How can I help you?"

It did not lend any help to my composure when the strange creature, with all her filmy garments settling gently around her, merely stood there staring at me. The starlight from the window caught her eyes and made them glitter. Tiring of this cat-and-mouse game, I stepped back into the sitting room, lighted my candle at the grate, and with the little flame rising brightly and cheerfully, my bedchamber appeared far less sinister. Its unwelcome occupant, however, did not even blink in that light, which must have been a genuine shock after the darkness of the chapel steps.

Lucie took a few tentative steps toward me, her large eyes seeming to see through me. Her soft voice murmured wistfully, "Rachel dear, do be the good, sweet thing that you are, and help me."

We were now in reversed positions, and I, not liking it too well, found my back to the open door of the chapel steps.

With as quiet and calm a voice as I could muster, I said, "Miss Lucie, Rachel is gone. You sent her away." I paused, saw that she had not taken that glassy gaze from me, and ventured then, "Miss Lucie . . . Where is Mrs. Herrenrath? Now. At this precise minute."

This time, her eyelids did flicker. Her faint, pale eyebrows raised, and although I could not be sure without lifting the candle higher, it appeared that thc pupils of her eyes dilated. I tried to read in these symptoms the horrid possibility that she had been awake and fully aware during all the time I saw her crossing the Great Hall and after, when she stood in this room in the dark, waiting for me.

"Is it Anne?" she asked, her voice trailing upward vaguely. "I need your help. Will you come with me?"

"Where?" The question was as flat as I could make it. Her eyelids fluttered again, and I felt she must be herself or she would have gone on calling me "Rachel."

"You know where. You know everything that goes on at Mist House. I need you. I'm in such dreadful trouble. Such . . ." her voice went up again, indistinct and faint, "dreadful trouble."

She swayed, raised both hands toward me, and then, as I put out my free hand, thinking to steady her, her gaze seemed to tighten, to fix on my hand with sudden intelligence. Before I could touch her, she opened her mouth and nearly deafened me with a wild shriek that must have echoed and reechoed throughout the great house. My first reaction was to set the candle down and my second, to cover my ears. But as she shrieked again and kept pointing her finger at me, I lost all sense of fitness and position. I slapped her roundly across the cheek.

She staggered, as I supposed under the cruel strength of that blow, and I caught her when she fell and seated her in the little chair nearby. It had been a shocking act, and I could only explain it as motivated by my own panic at her behavior. Seeing that she was still faint, I pushed her head down as gently as I could, and told her, "Keep your head down, ma'am. You'll feel better in just a few seconds."

I heard a step in the sitting room and looked around. Remembering, my stupid, thoughtless conduct, I was almost ashamed to meet Richard Dalreagh's eyes as he came into the bedchamber, frowning at the two of us. I thought briefly how curious it was that he was still fully dressed at this hour.

"What in the name of God is the matter? Has she completely lost her senses? Half the house is aroused. God knows what those cackling geese will think."

"I'm sorry, sir. I'm so sorry," I repeated as I looked around and up at him.

He joined me then, raising Lucie's head by her chin, asking me again, "What happened? I suppose she was sleepwalking as usual." I nodded. "And I've no doubt it was she who screamed."

"Yes. I'll get her some water." I rose from my knees and got the glass from my bedstand. The Earl put it to her lips, and she drank in convulsive gulps.

"I struck her," I said. "I was so—shocked when she began to scream. I was appalled, and I—"

"Never mind. I understand."

He took the glass away from her and handed it to me. While I was replacing it on the bedstand, I glanced over at the open door beside the bed. I confess it did not steady my nerves to see the chapel steps partially revealed by the candlelight. They looked to me like the teeth in a gigantic black mouth, and I was about to close the door when the Earl called me to Lucie's side.

"She is coming around. What really happened? What is she doing in your room?"

"I have no notion, my Lord. She came up from the chapel, I believe. I first saw her in the doorway there. No!" I remembered then and explained that I thought she had been sleepwalking across the Great Hall earlier.

"Probably. She has been like this since my brother died. She loved him as deeply, I suppose, as it is possible for a creature of her frailty to love anyone."

I was astonished at this observation by a man normally as intelligent as Lord Richard, but I tried not to let my doubts show in my face.

He looked at me, faintly smiling. "You have certainly had a baptism of terror since you happened on this madhouse. Will you be wishing to run away and leave us all in our bedlam?"

I told him sincerely, "I feel that its problems are now mine as well, sir. I should find it difficult, indeed, to leave you—to leave Mist House now before I know the cause of its troubles."

He touched my hand, said quietly, "Thank you, dear Anne," and turned his attention to Lucie. She began to straighten her spine, to sit up, cringing away from her brother-in-law. She still shook with a kind of palsied terror.

"Don't touch me, please. I shall be well presently, when I am safe, when I know, of a certainty . . . Anne, help me to get back."

Disgusted with what he must have considered her absurd antipathy, the Earl stood up and said impatiently, "Very well, then. Anne, would you be so good as to take her to her apartment?"

I had a feeling that she was not asking me to help her to her bedchamber, but rather to some other room, less pleasant and probably less safe. As I was taking her by the arm to get her on her feet, the Earl walked into the sitting room, and then I heard the sounds out in the corridor beyond, the buzz of many people, padded footsteps, muffled male voices punctuated by the higher-pitched twitter of females. I was following close behind the Earl, and he looked around at me. He grimaced.

"Oh Lord! She's roused the household. Well, come along. We'll simply say we found her sleepwalking."

A stout, bald man in a ludicrous black dressing robe festooned with red dragons peeked around the partially open sitting room door.

"Ah, Dick! There you are. I say, there's been a frightful row. Creatures screaming—dreadful business!"

"Yes, yes, Horace." The Earl dismissed the matter impatiently. "Mrs. Dalreagh is a somnambulist, as I am sure you have heard. She woke up in unnecessary terrcr. She is in the very good hands of Miss Killain, our housekeeper. There will be no more disturbances tonight."

I devoutly hoped not.

I had heard my husband tell me that Indians in the Americas often make their captives run a gauntlet. It was rather like a gauntlet that we faced as Lucie and I began our walk down the Long Gallery. There were more than a dozen persons, among them a white-faced Louis Minotte, and even two or three personal ladies' maids who stared at us and then buzzed like noisy insects. Lucie hunched down as if to hide between me and those curious, staring eyes.

"You're very brave, Anne," she said in her soft, only half-audible voice, which she used at certain specified times.

"They won't hurt you. They are your friends."

"I don't mean that. I mean in your bedchamber a little while ago. When I screamed . . . Why d'you think I screamed?"

I remembered very well why she screamed. She had been staring at me as I stood by the open door to the chapel steps, and when I put out my hand to help her, she pointed a finger at me and shrieked loudly enough to be heard by all these people in every corner of the ancient house.

"You were pointing at me when you screamed, ma'am. I've no doubt something about me startled you." I spoke barely above a whisper to prevent our conversation from being overheard by the guests. They kept milling around, undecided whether to follow the Earl's advice to return to bed or to continue addressing their unanswered questions to their disheveled hostess:

"Mrs. Dalreagh, are you quite well?"

"Dear Lucie, is there anything I may do? My maid is very competent. I am persuaded she could make you a warm posset that would put you sound asleep in no time."

To the latter formidable lady, I expressed Lucie's thanks and refusal, which Lucie cut into by raising her voice and saying as she shook my arm, "You don't understand at all, Anne. It wasn't you I pointed to, and it wasn't something about you that startled me. And not startled—*terrorized,* Anne! Just behind you, in that open doorway of the chapel steps, where I had been only minutes before, was the Black Abbess herself. That awful creature. She was standing—or seemed to be standing—so close behind you she could have touched you if I had not screamed."

Holy Mary, Mother of God!

I think at that minute I came my closest, thus far, to a shriek that would have done justice to Lucie's banshee wails. All during those moments when I thought I was fighting Lucie's strong hysterics, that phantom, the "creature who did not exist," *might* have been looming there at my back. Even now, when Lucie told me, I felt the ghastly chill, the gooseflesh over my body.

"When did it disappear?" I asked after I could control my voice. At least, we were beyond the eavesdropping, buzzing guests. We could talk between ourselves.

She shook her head vaguely.

"I don't know. Sometime while I was feeling so faint." She looked up at me with the hopeful stare of a child. "Do you think? . . . Perhaps my screams did frighten it away. Do you think it is possible?"

"Very possible. You may well have saved my life."

She smiled gratefully. We had reached the door to her sitting room, and I opened it and watched her flutter in, to fall on a chaise longue covered in pink satin, exactly suited to the woman Lucie seemed to be. She looked up again, though, when I asked her if I should send her maid to her.

"Not unless she is here, thank you, Anne. I . . . I think I would like to be alone. It's been a hectic time, and I want just to lie here and remember my—my husband."

I was so surprised at this that I nearly betrayed my feeling.

"Mister—Kevin? Yes, of course." And then I remembered the stories, the hints of his suffering, the last moments which Dr. Malcolm said were so painful. I thought back over the conversation the day before between the surgeon and me. "You loved him very much, His Lordship tells me."

She turned up her nose disdainfully.

"Much Richard knows. He'd not believe me if I lay in my coffin." I turned to go, and she said with a kind of urgency that impressed me, "All the same, I loved Kevin from the first moment Mama introduced us. It was at an Assembly Ball. He danced very badly, but he was so big, so—" I had a horrid feeling she would cry, but she finished with only the sad little refrain, "so very dear. You see, Anne, it was not his fault he changed so much and became so irritable before he died. It was the fall he took. I don't know how he came to do so. But he was a bruising rider."

I said, "Yes. Good night, ma'am," and was vastly relieved to see her maid hurrying along the corridor toward Lucie's open door. I called to her, asked the girl to see Mrs. Dalreagh and went back through the Long Gallery toward my own rooms. Since Lucie and I came through that corridor, most of the guests and their servants had returned to the guests chambers, for which I was profoundly grateful. It had been embarrassing enough to be seen even once in my night garments on the long walk to Lucie's chamber. I hurried through the gallery on my return trip and was only forced to pause twice in order to make my respectful curtsy. The first time was to the heavy man in the dragon night robe, and I was just rising from that curtsy when Lord Richard came along toward us from the direction of the chapel steps and my rooms.

The fat gentleman rolled his eyes, made some remark about "Irish looks," and for an instant, I thought he would try to kiss me. I backed away with unflattering haste, but the gentleman and I were both surprised when His Lordship took a long stride, came between us and said in a dreadfully rude voice, "Horace, you are far from your bedchamber. Shall I ring for a servant to lead you there?"

"Dear me, no!" said the gentleman, more politely than the words deserved. "I'm off this moment, Dick, old man. This moment." He winked gaily at me. "Old Horace Wimblesley knows when he's treading on other toes, eh, my pretty colleen?"

"Horace, that Madeira was more potent than I thought," said His Lordship, thus capping his rudeness as well as Sir Horace's opinion of our relationship.

I started to say something, but there was no protest I could make that would not call renewed attention to Sir Horace's humiliating mistake. By the time he had padded down the gallery on feet ridiculously small for his girth, Richard was saying to me, "I'll see you back to your room."

I glanced after Sir Horace, feeling my face

flame at the insulting things that would be said of me by the time that gentleman had brought his tale to the rest of the guests.

"Please, sir, you heard him. You must be aware of what will be said about me. I cannot be seen in the company of a gentleman like yourself at this hour." He was standing in such a way that I could not move without touching him. The gallery light someone had set burning at the end of the corridor left His Lordship's face in shadow, and I could not read it, but when I looked up at his eyes, I felt the attraction he had held for me from our first hour together—and I knew, too, how dangerous this would be, in view of our respective positions and the gossip that must already have started.

"My Lord, please!"

"Richard."

"My Lord Richard . . ."

He made a shrugging gesture of impatience at what he must have conceived to be my stupidity. Then suddenly, he was struck by the humor of my insistence on a formal relationship, and he laughed.

"Anne, Anne, forgive me. I am behaving like Horace. But you do enchant me. I have never known a girl like you before. Where do you come from? The end of the world?"

"From Ireland, sir."

He laughed again and stepped aside.

"Well then, to please you, I shall be circumspect. For the moment."

He made no motion to touch me as I curtsyed and passed him, going on my way, my head whirling with thoughts of him. Forbidden thoughts. Nothing could be more evident than that his interest in me was the cheap, sensual interest of a great lord for one of his serving women. I must never forget that.

I came to my sitting room, which was only faintly lighted by rays from the candle in my bedchamber. In that bedchamber, I knew I would find the door to the chapel steps still open, as it had been when the Black Abbess stood there silently at my back. I had not seen her; yet, I knew with a terrible, sure sense of its truth that *someone* had been there and that only Lucie's scream had saved me from his or her horrible touch.

13

I paused in sudden panic before going through the doorway into the room. At the same time, I was deeply conscious of my own cowardice. I knew I dreaded seeing those chapel steps through the open door that was so like a mouth to my imagination. That imagination was now more highly sensitized by the recent events of the night. My own knowledge of these cowardly qualms put me on my mettle. I walked into my bedroom with my fists clenched and every muscle set for action. In my mind was the thought, and the fear, that the ghostly Abbess or her impersonator was still there in the doorway, waiting for me. It was not dispelled until I had looked into every corner of the bedroom, including the clothespress, and climaxing with that dark flight of chapel steps. There was nothing in the doorway. It had been an absurd fear, I told myself, just as the notion of some strange, floating ghost was absurd. What had happened to my common sense that I should be so easily swayed by Lucie's idiocy?

I walked firmly to the chapel steps and peered down the plunging flight. Just for an instant, I thought something stirred in the darkness at the foot of the steps. I stepped back, took up the bedcandle, and held it high as I stood on the top step. Its flame illuminated the entire first flight as far as the turn at the second story. Nothing was there. Either the thing I fancied I saw was another imaginary floating object or it had descended to the next flight of steps.

Furious with my own repeated susceptibility, I stepped back into the bedchamber and slammed the door shut, bolting it with all my force.

"This is the last time I'll be opening that door," I promised myself angrily.

I went back to bed and, curiously enough, slept peacefully and dreamlessly until a little after sunrise, or as near to sunrise as one could expect that rainy morning. But I awoke to the fears of the previous night. My first act, on opening my eyes, was to glance over at the bolted door. The eternal drafts throughout the house swept up under the door, so that the sturdy timber seemed to move faintly now and then, as though it were breathing.

Unpleasant thought. I got up hastily and took up the tea tray whose arrival outside my sitting room door had awakened me. The hot tea was welcome on this cold, gloomy morning, and I felt infinitely better when I had set the tray on the table and begun to dress for the day ahead.

Due to the affairs of the night as well as the darkness of the stormy day, the morning began late for most of the Dalreagh funeral guests, and I was able to set the servants to work putting candelabra about on small tables or tabarets in each corridor of the three floors, as well as in the chapel and in the crypt. With these went firm instructions that each and every candle and every lamp should be lighted at dusk without fail. There were protests and threats of mutiny about the crypt task, and in the end, I was forced to lead the way so that they would enter the unpleasant if spacious place at all.

When the parlor maid and the second footman had departed, both protesting "this place of phantoms" was not in their domain as servants of the upper regions, I walked around the long, high-ceilinged hall, trying to imagine why it would have taken more courage than I possessed to come down here last night and face whatever had frightened Lucie in the open doorway of the chapel steps. How strong must the inducement have been to bring me down at that moment after I returned to my room, when I stood on the top of the chapel steps and imagined I saw some faint movement at the foot of those stairs that looked merely historic and badly worn!

I walked from one end of the crypt to the other. The hall was partly illuminated by a bluish light filtering in through the high, small apertures that served as windows. It was not in any sense fully lighted, and I was surprised to find Miss Amanda busy at work in her accustomed place at the far end of the crypt, which received the least illumination. Nor did she have a candle with her. Her short, strong hands were buried in some sort of gray-pink substance which I took to be clay, and the head she had been shaping the previous night was a trifle more perfect, more smooth. I assumed she had accomplished this in the early morning. It was scarcely midmorning now, and I said, hoping to mollify her after her hysterical outburst early the night before, "You are extraordinarily talented, Miss Amanda. Have you displayed your work in any way?" I was thinking, of course, of certain historic exhibits I had heard of in London, and more especially of strange and exotic items brought back to France in the wake of General Bonaparte's Egyptian campaign.

"I? Now, how should I display my work, as you call it? Do you take me for a street beggar?"

"Not at all," I said, understanding her proud attitude, but a trifle annoyed that nothing seemed to break her dislike of me. "It is only that the person my husband called 'the greatest man of our century' believed the display of art was a credit to a nation."

She glanced up at me curiously, and I realized, to my surprise, that for this short time I had managed after all to conquer her determined dislike of me.

"Then your husband was a Bonapartist, was he not?"

I nodded, and she went on, with a glow in her eyes that did wonders for her looks, "My tutor—that is, Monsieur Minotte—was a Bonapartist. It is very dangerous to be so these days, he says."

"Dangerous enough." It was a subject that still reminded me too painfully of my loss, though that time was more than two years past, and when Miss Amanda sat back and studied the statues that loomed over her on three sides, I was relieved to see that her interest was now directed at them.

"I did the small sister in the corner where the vaulting comes down low. It took me forever. Father taught me. In the end, I was better than he was, though."

I could believe it, looking at the figure she pointed to. The slender, sexless creature's robes were exquisitely arranged so that each fold had a special kind of grace. At first glance,

I had taken it for stone, like many of the others.

"Who do you suppose she was, the little nun?" Amanda asked dreamily. "Surely, there was a man for her, back in the thirteenth century."

"Perhaps, she felt the Church was her vocation."

But Amanda shook her head. "No. It was a man. He went off to some crusade or other and never came back . . . Poor little nun . . ."

She worked some sort of gritty substance into the clay, and when she saw my interest, she explained briefly, "It hardens quicker. Helps to give these statues that stony look everyone thinks so fine. I did the prone body on that coffin lid you are leaning against." Suddenly aware that I had been leaning against a body entombed some five hundred years ago, I moved away abruptly, and she grinned. "It's quite dead, I assure you. The statue standing next to it I did when I was so sick with a fever that I don't even remember finishing it. I completed the whole thing while I was delirious."

"Remarkable!" I stepped between two coffins to stare up at the big statue. The woman was extraordinarily muscular for a female; after a careful study, I decided it was actually a monk. At least, the cassock and the hood suggested as much. As usual, the hollow eyes stared down at me in such a way as to hurry me from the spot.

Amanda laughed.

"That's only Old Brother Ambroise. Don't be alarmed. They are all harmless. Though sometimes I do have a feeling that one day they'll all come to life and surround us and . . . and . . . well, what can an army of the dead do, after all?"

Considerable—if one had a very powerful imagination, I thought. Excusing myself, I went on my way to see after the dinner and serving preparations. These were especially complicated that day, as the Great Hall was to be used to accommodate the funeral guests who had remained.

Monsieur Minotte and Lucie, looking very pale, passed through the hall while I was changing the silver and the elaborate Dalreagh plate service to their correct places at the long table, and he stopped to help me while, to my surprise, Lucie went on into the chapel without him.

I looked after her and remarked on her pallor.

"I hope Mrs. Dalreagh is well. She was very much disturbed last night."

He dropped a fork with a clang against a wine glass, picked both up, and replaced them with shaking fingers.

"It is of this Madame wishes me to speak.

She believes you do not know of her deep love for her late husband."

I looked my astonishment.

"But Monsieur Minotte, it is no concern of mine. I did not even know Miss Lucie's late husband."

"Nevertheless, she was exceedingly devoted to him. Without doubt, mademoiselle, you have noted my own devotion—no!—my adoration of this saintly woman, but it is not reciprocated. She has no one else to count on. No arm to uphold her."

"She has the arm of her brother-in-law," I reminded him. "And surely the arm of His Lordship is strong enough, even for Miss Lucie."

"That may be, but she is frightened of him. The poor little creature is terrified of Lord Richard. A formidable man, let me tell you, mademoiselle."

With more feeling than I had intended to betray, I corrected him, "An admirable man, monsieur. In every respect, the most admirable man I have known since—" I did not finish. I had seen a shadow cross the light of the candle sconces that were needed on this rainy day, and I was fairly sure we were overheard even before Richard Dalreagh's pleasantly amused voice addressed us both, but I felt uneasily that he was speaking to me alone.

"It isn't often an eavesdropper hears so lovely a defense of himself."

I curtsyed slightly, using the respectful gesture to keep my gaze averted from him. I was determined not to place myself in a position where he might fancy I encouraged him to some act that would humiliate me and degrade him.

"Pardon, my Lord," said the Frenchman with a certain stiffness. "It was most improper of us to mention you in this fashion. Or," he added hastily, "in any way, of course."

The Earl waved this aside as of no account.

"It's of no consequence. I was looking for you, Minotte."

I started to leave them, as the Frenchman looked uneasy, and I supposed their conversation was to be tête-à-tête, but His Lordship casually took my wrist without looking my way and held me there, an embarrassed observer.

"If I may be permitted to oblige Your Lordship," Louis Minotte began vaguely.

"Precisely. When will my niece be ready to be presented at the London Season?"

It was obvious that the tutor had been caught unawares; he appeared genuinely shocked. I tried not to understand why, but the truth leaped to my eyes. When Miss Amanda's education in the Courtly Graces was completed, Monsieur Minotte's service would no longer be required at Mist House. And the unfortunate man could hardly really teach Lucie Dalreagh *any* of the arts and Courtly Graces. I felt sure she was far more worldly from the moment of her birth, in most significant ways, than this perspiring and nervous young man. Louis Minotte would thus, very shortly, have no further excuse for remaining to defend his idolized Lucie. In some respects, I thought it tragic. They seemed ideally suited to each other.

"It is difficult to say when the young mademoiselle will be ready precisely, my Lord," he stammered. "She . . . she is not—that is to say, Miss Amanda's gifts and splendid qualities lie in other directions. She is an expert horsewoman, for example."

"But that is not in your curriculum, is it, Monsieur Minotte?" asked the Earl in an ironic voice that must have cut Louis Minotte's pride to ribbons.

"Quite true. Yet . . . yet . . ."

The Earl smiled. "Then you must hurry your teaching, must you not, monsieur?"

"I—I feel sure that if Your Lordship understood the entire . . . That is to say, you cannot imagine how very much I have tried—to be of assistance." Louis Minotte began to wring his hands, a gesture I had not thought to see outside the romances in which such gestures are cheaply come by. "Madame Dalreagh depends on my advice and my very respectful support in the difficult times ahead."

Involuntarily, I glanced at the Earl. His clasp upon my wrist had tightened until I moved my hand experimentally, trying to restore circulation in it.

"I am persuaded you think so, my dear Minotte. Now, I would suggest you set about making my niece ready for her presentation at Carlton House during the approaching London Season."

Monsieur Minotte bowed formally, at last, beginning to recover from these successive sharp *touchés* by an expert fencer.

"Very well, my Lord. I shall do whatever is in my power. I trust that—that Your Lordship will someday understand the delicacy, the helpless . . . sweet qualities of Lucie—of your brother's widow." He put his clenched fist to his forehead with another of those dreadful, theatrical gestures which, in another, I might have despised; but in Louis Minotte, they seemed supremely expressive, even poignant. "I implore you to be generous. Understanding."

He broke off as if exhausted, and while we stared at him, he suddenly pushed past us and started off almost on the run toward the chapel. I knew who was in the chapel, but when the Earl remarked, "Good Lord! What ails the fellow? What is he doing in the chapel?" I did not answer. Lord Richard shook my hand for emphasis, as he spoke, but did not release it. I said, after a moment, "If Your Lordship will excuse me, there are so many things to be done before your guests come in to dine."

"Anne," he said, suddenly not sardonic or smiling but with every appearance of sincerity, "Why are you so shy of me?" He added with one eyebrow raised, "I am not one of the Carlton House dandies, and I do not seduce respectable young ladies under my own roof. What is there about me that makes you recoil as though I were—God knows what?"

I was terribly conscious of my position, which was very much opposed by the mental as well as physical attraction he exerted on me. So much about him was like the only man I had ever loved that my heart felt as if it were squeezed between his two hands, and I scarcely knew which way to turn or to answer. I said, as steadily as I could, "You must know why I recoil, as you say . . . as Your Lordship says. Nevertheless, I feel a deep—admiration for you." It was the only word I could think of, and it was a feeble one, not nearly what I might have said in other circumstances, if our positions were equal. Raising my head and looking at him, I said more firmly, "Is that what you wished me to say?"

His free hand took my other wrist as well, so that I was imprisoned by one whose touch warmed my whole body and turned me weak with longing for the enjoyment of old sensations, old and forgotten tenderness.

"Don't!" I said hoarsely. "They murdered him. I won't live the anguish of love and lose it again. Not again!" I tried to pull away from him and, in doing so, forced him almost involuntarily to resist. This brought our bodies together, and in a way too heady and confusing for me to remember, he was kissing me, and I, instead of making further resistance, returned his kiss with all the passion I had so long reserved for my dreams and memories.

"Richard!" cried Lucie Dalreagh. "How could you? Not Anne! She was once a scullery maid. Did you know that?" She and the Frenchman had come up softly from the chapel.

I broke away from him, knowing then all the humiliation I had feared. The Earl was so furious, and perhaps startled, that for an instant he raised his hand, and Louis Minotte and I, the horrified witnesses, both cried out as he brought it down. Lucie cringed, but she was perfectly safe now. Richard said with icy contempt, "You little vixen! I know you poisoned my brother. Don't speak to me of scullery maids. You soil yourself. Not Anne. *You,* Minotte! Take her to—to wherever murderesses make their peace with their consciences."

Lucie's thin face quivered, and as the tutor took her gently to lead her away, she cried brokenly to Richard, "I didn't! I didn't! Oh, won't anyone believe me? Louis, tell him."

But there seemed nothing more to be said. I felt Lucie's desperate plea and believed her. But I was so obsessed with the awful scene, the actions and the words between the four of us, that I scarcely knew what my confused feelings were.

When the Frenchman had taken Lucie away, I stared in the opposite direction. I knew, even as I moved, that Lord Richard's eyes were on me, that he wanted to say something. But there was nothing to be said between us. He should have known, and I, worse culprit, *had* known the consequences of this impossible relationship.

"Anne?"

"I must leave here. You know that, my Lord."

I straightened my shoulders to give me both confidence and the old pride which I should never have lost.

"Not, surely, until you have arranged our lives, Anne. Yours and mine. Look on me as a man, not as—something my ancestors gave me. A stupid, constricting title which serves no purpose in the world whatever."

"It is considerably more than that, my Lord," I said, knowing perfectly well that his words, lovely and soothing though they might be, were not what he would be thinking ten hours from now.

"Anne."

I said, without looking around, "My Lord, that is unworthy, the pursuit of these gentlemanly tastes. You know there is no longer any place for me here. I am not high enough to be the wife to an Earl and not low enough to be his mistress. Good day, sir!"

14

"Miss Killain!" I recognized the voice of male authority, of my employer, and above all, of a person whose requests of me I should forever obey, within moral bounds.

"Yes, my Lord."

In three or four strides he was beside me. He did not touch me; yet, I felt, with all my heart, the closeness of him, the importance to me of his presence.

"Will you speak to me in your capacity as housekeeper?"

"With all my heart, sir. So long as I remain at Mist House."

"With all your heart? Well, perhaps not quite." He laughed without humor. "No matter. I want to talk to you. About the conditions here in this accursed house of death."

I turned then, at once.

"Sir, I swear to you that little chamber beside the crypt was filled with Mrs. Herrenrath's things two day ago. Why it should be nearly empty now, I can't begin to guess."

"Oh, that!" He waved away the mystery that

had so much troubled me. "There are a dozen reasons, all equally plausible, for the disappearance—or appearance—of her property, whichever troubles you most."

"What troubles me, my Lord, is where the lady may be at this minute."

He smiled and shook his head.

"I am reasonably certain the woman is off somewhere making difficulties for other households. She certainly made herself disliked here. Then, too, she has ordered certain of her property from time to time."

"Pardon me, sir, but how do you know that? Did she notify you personally?"

He had put out his arm to me politely as we came into the chapel and headed toward the steps to my room, but suddenly seemed to recall our recent near-quarrel and did not touch me. In other circumstances, I might have longed for the touch of his hand on mine, but so long as I remained at Mist House in my present capacity, I knew our relationship must remain strictly that of master and upper servant. Anything else would be disastrous.

"I don't suppose I ever thought twice about Rachel Herrenrath, Anne—Miss Killain, that is to say." He paused, went on then, carefully, as if on tiptoe. "You cut rather deep, you know. I kissed you because I very much desired to kiss you." I tried to interrupt, but he raised his hand in an imperative gesture whose authority

I obeyed. "I desired to kiss you because you are a desirable woman. I should have done the same thing had I felt the same desire for one of my guests here—Lady Horace, for example. Ah! You are smiling. That is better."

It was too ludicrous, picturing the Earl of Dalreagh seizing Sir Horace's elderly wife in some dark corner and squeezing all the enormous bulk of her. But he evaded the matter at hand.

"Don't you see, sir, there is something very strange about Mrs. Herrenrath. I sometimes wonder if anyone in Mist House has seen her since she was dismissed."

All the light camaraderie between us disappeared, and I was both sorry and relieved. He stopped as we crossed the center of the chapel, and glanced over at the altar where Lucie was kneeling while Monsieur Minotte stood beside her with one hand outstretched, as if entreating her.

Richard frowned, hunting for a memory. Then he said to me briskly, "I dismissed the woman and gave her several months' salary. But I have had no concern about her since. However . . ."

He left my side and crossed the chapel to the two at the altar. The Frenchman looked at him indignantly.

"Your Lordship cannot seriously contemplate interrupting Madame at her prayers."

"That I cannot say. Unless she knows something about Rachel Herrenrath."

Lucie's head jerked up and the chapel resounded with an abrupt little crash as her *Book of Common Prayer* slipped from her fingers and fell to the stones just beyond the red carpeting. But it was Louis Minotte who spoke at once, with hauteur.

"Madame knows nothing of the woman. It is I who—"

"Yes?" The Earl prompted him so pleasantly I shivered at the ironic quality of the single word.

The pallor of the Frenchman seemed accentuated. More than ever, he reminded me of those theatrical young gentlemen, so prevalent in London now, who hoped their black hair and romantic pallor would remind someone of the famous, or infamous, Lord Byron.

"It is true. It was I who brought Madame Herrenrath's boxes to her in the village."

I knew it was imprudent, and further, it was rude to show them that I had overheard them, but speaking across what seemed to me the great space of the chapel interior, I said, "Forgive me, monsieur, but when did you take those boxes to Mrs. Herrenrath?"

"Why, yesterday," Louis Minotte looked around at each of us. "It was well known by the staff of the house."

"Not yesterday, I think, monsieur," I reminded him. "The cook's son saw you on your way into the village, unencumbered. And quite early, I saw the housekeeper's property. It filled the storage chamber."

Louis Minotte said hastily, "Jeremiah is mistaken. I took Rachel's things to her much later—in the morning."

Lucie had reached up and plucked at his coat sleeve. I could imagine the desperate plea in her eyes, and I wondered, terribly concerned.

She murmured, loudly enough for me to hear in the big, hollow room, "He did! I know Louis took the things in to town to oblige that horrid woman . . . Anne, you remember. You spoke of it."

I stepped farther into the room toward the three, who were gathered at the other end under the big, beamed roof. The Earl motioned to me, but I took only a few steps, then stopped.

"Miss Lucie, nothing was removed from the crypt chamber until last night. I am persuaded His Lordship means merely to ask why the property of Mrs. Herrenrath remained until late yesterday afternoon and then was removed."

She looked around at Louis Minotte and then at the Earl, her face strained with the tension of whatever problem ailed her.

"But I thought—all this while I have believed that Rachel demanded but one box at a time and that her portmanteaus and bandboxes were delivered to her in that order, as she called on someone for them."

I did not utter the question that troubled me throughout this unpleasant interview. I was well aware that I had precipitated the questions and that without the incitement on my part, the Earl would not have thought to question the curious business of Mrs. Herrenrath's disappearance. But the Earl himself now seemed to have guessed what puzzled and worried me so much. He had none of my reluctance to ask pertinent and perhaps even deadly questions.

"Minotte, you may as well tell me now and save a great deal of bother in future. When did Rachel Herrenrath ask for the return of her cases and where was she when she asked for them?"

"But monsieur, she . . . sent a boy to Mist House with the message. I happened to be present at that time and replied, as seemed most convenient, with the property she asked to be delivered to her. Quite simple, harming no one. You comprehend, my Lord?"

The Earl said, "I am beginning to . . . I think. Go on. Give me the details."

"That is all, my Lord," the harassed Frenchman insisted eagerly. "I delivered nearly all of her property to—" He paused.

"Well?" asked the Earl.

"To the boy who met me at the coach stop, in the village," Monsieur Minotte finished. He was sweating profusely. Even I could see that.

"Then, the woman was leaving by coach. Accommodation Coach, Mail Coach? Or what?"

"The—the Accommodation Coach, I believe. The boy told me he had been asked to guard the lady's property until she came out and mounted the coach."

"Oh. Then she was bound for London. You did say this was last evening?"

"Yes, my Lord. Last evening. And, alas! London is such a very large place in which to locate a person."

"What time in the evening?"

"Rather late. That is to say, nine, perhaps."

I started to say something but fortunately kept silent. The Earl was staring at Minotte in a way that would have chilled me had I been the recipient of that look.

"The Accommodation Coach at that hour goes north, not south. And not to London."

"Does it?" Minotte licked his lip and then said immediately after, "I must have been mistaken in the direction. I suppose the coach turned or something of that sort. As a matter of fact, I did not wait to see it, so very likely it was the northbound coach, after all."

"I believe," said the Earl calmly, "I shall go into the village tomorrow and talk with those who saw Rachel Herrenrath since I gave her quittance along with the money. She is a very officious woman, as I recall, and I shouldn't think there would be much difficulty in finding some few who remember her presence in the village these past weeks . . . And now, Lucie, you had best stop sniveling and make preparations to entertain your dinner guests."

"I was not sniveling!" She came back with surprising fire and indignation. "I was praying."

"Well, well, whatever it was, you had best be on your way."

Being in the background and unperceived by the three of them at the moment, I took his warning to apply to me as well and left the chapel quietly while the others were still there. I walked up the chapel steps to the top of the third flight, tried my bedchamber door, which was tight-bolted as I had left it, and went through the corridor door instead, arriving in my apartment by means of the sitting room door.

I went at once to the clothespress and studied the spot far to the back where Mrs. Herrenrath's clothes had hung. They were, of course, gone now, but I hoped some idea would come to me, some reasonable explanation for her having left them. One rather obvious one loomed up: She had received money from an unexpected—or expected?—source and decided to buy an entire new wardrobe. But the salary paid to her by the Earl was hardly great enough to make her throw aside all her property. Besides, it was only the money she would have expected to receive during her normal tenure at Mist House. And she would be extremely improvident if she spent it all in this fashion . . . *unless* she expected or had received money from another source.

I closed the doors of the old-fashioned press and went to the window, leaning my cheek against the cold glass while I considered. It was perfectly possible that she had discovered a secret involving a member of the Dalreagh family; for one thing they all, even the servants, agreed upon—she was forever prying and spying. I could not acquit myself of this annoying habit, but at least, I did not demand payment for what I discovered.

There was work to do, and I could not stand about all evening conjuring up mysteries which involved a woman now legitimately gone for several weeks. I set about the various tasks, ate dinner with the staff, and went to bed early that night, hoping there would be no more of the nerve-racking interferences which had affected my previous nights.

My sleep was uninterrupted, and as a result, my nerves should have been completely calm. Most of the funeral guests departed after a late, lavish breakfast, and those who remained at Mist House set out on a hunt over the still-wet fields to the south. I had supposed that Miss Amanda was not socially inclined, but I was pleased to notice that she was aware of her best physical attributes and rode off at the head of the little group, with Louis Minotte and Lucie riding somewhat in her wake.

While the hunt left Mist House empty of gentlefolk—for the Earl had ridden off early to the village—the servants and I changed and remade the beds, cleaned guest rooms, and changed a number of the carpets throughout the big house. We reached the chapel's worn and dusty strip of red carpet sometime after noon and managed to do a thorough job of the huge, high-ceilinged hall. I doubt if the vaults and beams had been cleaned before within the memory of any then living.

It was not until much later that a noisy rumble of voices came to us from the guardroom, which had been my first sight of the interior of Mist House that night of my arrival. I sent the scullery maid to find out the trouble, and she seemed to get waylaid somehow. I went across to see what the trouble was myself, and found the ladies' maid, Phoebe, loudly contesting a dark, dripping brown object which I at first mistook for an animal. The cook's lanky redheaded son, Jeremiah, had the other end of the dripping object, and the tug of war threatened to reach every member of the household.

"Give it me! Madam should see it!" the girl cried shrilly.

"No! It's the master's business. Or—" Jeremiah caught sight of me and tried to wave the brown object. "Mum, 'tis me that found it, and all like it, in the moat. His Lordship will be cross as sticks if it ain't left to his notice."

"I'm sure you are right," I told him, but in a voice that I hoped would not further ruffle the situation. "Perhaps we can leave it in some safe place for His Lordship's examination upon his return."

"We can't, ma'am. We just can't!" the girl sobbed. "It'll be Mrs. Dalreagh's cloak. I've my orders."

I looked at the wet lump of material, held it up between the three of us, and saw that it actually was a woman's cloak and that it unquestionably looked familiar. The longer I studied it, the more familiar it looked. I had used exactly such a cloak in which to wrap Mrs. Herrenrath's property. Somewhere along the hem, the threads had been torn. I ran my fingers over the hem. The threads were torn.

I said to Phoebe, "You may go," and then to Jeremiah, "You found this in the moat? Was this all you found?"

"No, mum. There's a deal more. All wound around the bridge pilings. It's a miracle it didn't float downstream, but the water rose so high in the storm yesterday, and I expect it brought down a deal of brush and whatnot. So everything's tangled up in it now."

This explained the sudden disappearance of nearly everything in that storage chamber.

"Jeremiah, take the stableboy and bring me everything you can conveniently reach from the bridge. But please—don't fall in."

"A bit oddlike, ain't it, mum?"

"Very." I did not ask that he also keep an eye out for any floating bodies he might come upon, but the thought did cross my mind, and I went out and examined the moat and river myself. Nothing of that sort was visible, however, for which I was exceedingly grateful.

By the time he had returned with the great loads of muddy, saturated clothing and other items, I had cleared a place for them in the guardroom and asked two of the outside boys to take turns watching it. I felt it vastly important that the Earl should see this and perhaps solve the curious mystery of Rachel Herrenrath.

I was not surprised, however, late in the evening, to be told that the two boys were not only afraid to guard the property singly but also in pairs.

"What seems to be the trouble?" I asked the parlor maid, who had been delegated to inform me of this latest domestic contretemps.

" 'Tis the Abbess, mum. The lads is forever a-feared the Abbess will come a-floatin' up out of the crypt. They be fair close to the crypt steps, as ye may know."

"I do know, perfectly well." I sighed. I was tired in every bone and muscle, but there would be no peace until something was done to keep that wretched woman's property safe for Richard Dalreagh's examination. I went down again to the guardroom and ordered the boys to bring the untidy pile to the storage chamber.

"N-no, Mum, if ye please! No' but I'd oblige in any other way. Not the crypt."

I turned to the other boy, all of whose freckles stood out in separate protest.

"Nor me. Nor me, mum!"

It ended by my sending both boys off to the stables with hints of impending dismissal if they continued to be so cowardly. I bundled up as large a pile of clothing as I could carry and went through the Great Hall, which was empty, and down the stone steps. I unlocked the now-familiar closet, replaced the housekeeper's property, all the time considering and dismissing various possibilities—among them, the horrid thought that Rachel Herrenrath herself may never have left Mist House.

I made several trips, each time keenly aware of the draft blowing through the open archway of the crypt close behind me. My orders had been obeyed the previous night, and the candles lighted at dusk. Tonight, cowardice won. The crypt was dark again. I tried to conquer that absurd and childish fear by concentrating on a possible hiding place for the housekeeper's body. If she had been murdered for some reason, the cause seemed perfectly simple. Her spying had gained her a dangerous knowledge.

Just as I was locking the storage chamber, I remembered the unlighted candles in the crypt and took up the shielded lamp from the newel post, intending to light the candles myself. It was surprising how very much of a draft there was, though the weather outside had been mild since the rain. Probably behind some pillar or statue in the crypt there was a door. It was a logical notion. Otherwise, there would have been difficulty in bringing the bodies of the dead *religieuses* to this place.

No matter. I was beginning to feel a sympathy for the cowardice of the stableboys. I stepped through the archway, lighting the first candle just inside the crypt.

It was curious how strong the sensation was that I was not alone in the great vault. Naturally, I told myself, as I raised the protected candle, I was not alone. The place was populated with these insidiously alive stone images. I seemed to be surrounded by an army of the dead, all staring at me out of those dreadful eyes with empty sockets. I tried to light a second candle, and my fingers shook. Heartily ashamed of myself, I tried again. A distinct draft blew the flame out as rapidly as I lighted it. Could it be possible that Amanda was down here, as she had been that other night, having fallen asleep in her work?

I went rapidly to that end of the crypt, found much of her property still here where she had left it sometime today or yesterday, and was now more than ever sensitive to those stone guardians between me and the archway where I had entered the crypt. Another little draft blew out the candle flame I had already established and nearly plunged me in darkness. Thrown off my balance by the shock of trying to protect the candle in my hand, I reached, almost unconsciously, for the solid protection of one of the big statues.

Two things happened at once. A shadow crossed the archway, and my astounded eyes thought they saw in that archway a tall, heavily robed and coifed nun, all in black but for the bandeau that outlined the blurred and shadowy face. I screamed and dug my fingers hard into the statue that loomed close above me . . . and bits of the statue crumbled off in my hands. The Abbess was gone that quickly. I turned my head to stare, unbelieving, at the statue, and when I looked back, there was nothing in the archway. But beneath the clay and gritty material of the statue, my fingers had touched a cold, yielding, waxy substance that might have been human flesh.

15

I now felt fairly sure that I knew where Rachel Herrenrath was and why she had not removed her property. I peeled away a few more bits of clay and large, crumbling slices of the substance Amanda said she used to harden the figures . . .

Amanda! Where was she? What did she know of this particular statue?

While my mind considered the hideous fact very calmly, almost numbly, my emotions were gathered in my stifling chest as I glanced again at the archway, my only conceivable exit from the huge crypt. Whatever, or whoever, had stood there a moment before was gone now, and still I did not quite have the courage to walk over and peer around in the dark beyond the lamplight, where the creature might be hiding now, if it had not been a figment of my horrified imagination.

I gave a sidelong glance at the statue towering above me and then raised my lamp. Whatever was within that mixture of clay and God-knows-what appeared to have the color of flesh long dead and ill-preserved. I could see only a small circle of that flesh, even in the light, but I could not be mistaken. My life has had its distasteful moments, its ugly tasks: I know death and rotting flesh.

I looked away. This *was* Amanda's province. Amanda would know how this thing could have been contrived and could advise me, pending the arrival of the Earl.

God in heaven! Very probably, *only* Amanda could have done this!

My hand was shaking, and I lowered the lamp. Something I had done in touching the statue, or perhaps the chilling draft which wound through the crypt, made the big statue waver. I leaped back quickly, guessing what was to follow, and as the great creature toppled toward me, a huge gray shaft with death at its core, my own escape was threatened. In my frantic effort to escape its fall, I stumbled backward over the low stool which was Amanda's seat when she worked there. I fell in a twisted bundle of painfully bruised arms and legs, just as the statue shattered around me, showering me with bits of clay—and what was left of a human arm.

I suppose I must have screamed again, but I did not hear the sound, only the falling bits of clay and plaster and even some of the wall, which chipped away as it was struck. I was scrambling to get to my feet when, once more, a shadow passed before the candle at the archway, and I knew that I was not alone in the crypt. When I tried to resume my struggle, the remains of that once-human hand and arm lay now across my lap, and I lacked all power to free myself. The slight weight of that thing did not hold me, but something had happened to my nerves and my will. I stared at the debris.

Except for that partially uncovered arm and hand, which would look like almost anything but human flesh to a person inexperienced in such matters, most of the statue was still intact. The clay was cracked, broken off in many places, but the very fact that it had coated and protected the body beneath kept it fairly close to its original form. I tried again to get to my feet, encumbered by my skirts as well as the debris, and as I stood up, I brushed frantically at every shred of clay and the grit and sand that had also showered me.

Finally, knowing I must, I kneeled and touched first the cracked and broken clay, then the slivers of skin revealed between their dry covering. I felt a shudder suffuse my body with gooseflesh. As I exposed more of it, I became convinced that my first supposition had been correct. The hand was that of a woman of middle age, the pudgy fingers surprisingly well preserved. I bolstered my nerve and chipped away a bit of the clay about the face. But I could not go on. A first small glimpse of the skull was too much.

Could Amanda have done this? A girl so young? Surely not. Her talent in this field of clay and stone was unusual. Her wrists were strong. Physically, she was capable of murder. Yet, the evidence was almost too obvious. But most damning of all, who else had the talent and knowledge of the art to form this obscene and terrible travesty of a once living woman?

Instinctively, I looked over my shoulder at the rest of the stone monsters. I had the sudden, mad thought that perhaps other bodies were concealed within these shadowy, watching figures. The lamp's uneasy glow was such that I did not, at first, realize the faint movement now in the shadows beyond the archway. Whatever I had sensed there when I was still confused and battered by the collapse of the statue seemed not to have retreated while I was examining the uncovered portions of the woman's body.

I got to my feet painfully knowing I must get help, and threaded my way across the vault among the ancient coffins, aware again, but without applying my mind to it, that between the stones stagnant water was still gathered in little runnels.

Something moved suddenly near the storage chamber and then, in a flutter of what appered to be black robes, seemed to float up the steps to the chapel, where it became a part of the general darkness. Was this, at last, to be my direct encounter with the Black Abbess?

I knew a quick, burning fury as I took up one of the extra candlesticks with a hard metal base, pinched out the flame, and turned it upside down to use as a weapon. Then, I hurried out of the crypt and up the steps after the creature. I had not seen the face or even the exact contours, but this was my only chance to face it down, and I did not intend to miss it or allow it to commit more depredations. If the Black Abbess were a member of the Dalreagh household, as seemed most likely, either one of the gentry or a servant, I would now know which within minutes.

At the top of the steps, I was confused for an instant, though no less furious, when I thought I had lost the Abbess. Then, I saw the guardroom door close, and I followed quickly. The guardroom was empty, but I could see the indistinct figure in its dark, fluttering skirt or habit as it hurried across the inner courtyard beyond the fountain.

"Stop!" I cried with every iota of authority I possessed. I hardly expected a response to my command, but I called out again. At the very least, I had satisfied myself that the Abbess, if this creature was the Abbess, was no phantom, but flesh and blood. By this time, I was close behind. As we reached the far door that opened out of the courtyard on a little passage that ran through the house and onto the insecure board bridge to the family graveyard, I slammed shut the door just as my quarry opened it, so that the Abbess was trapped beside me.

"Now then," I said, holding high the lamp with its protective shield while the other hand was busy with my heavy, sharp weapon, "Let us see our precious ghost."

I suspected as soon as the light flashed upward in the open air that there were differences between this person, attempting so strenuously to conceal his or her identity, and the silent creature who had watched me from the deep shadow outside the crypt. But by this time, it was too late to stop myself from thrusting back the hood of a wide, enveloping storm cloak.

The hood thrown back brought down Amanda Dalreagh's heavy hair, which had been thrust up, carelessly, on top of her head and fastened by several hair bodkins.

"Let me go!" she whispered tightly through set teeth. "Don't you understand? He's running away. Running away . . . and I can't stop him."

"Miss Amanda! I thought it was that accursed Abbess." In fact, I knew perfectly well that the Abbess had been my first quarry, and then, somewhere—probably when I went running through the guardroom—I had lost my trail of the real Black Abbess and stumbled on

Amanda. But even as I framed an apology to the girl, I was wondering if, just possibly, Amanda really was the Black Abbess and had, somehow, changed an outer robe, a habit, and allowed herself to be trapped in all her indignant and protested innocence.

"He's gone, you fool!" she cried, much more loudly, no longer aware of any who might overhear. "You've made me lose him."

"Who was it?" I asked, ready to question her about the real horror, to force the confession that she knew about Rachel Herrenrath's body.

"But, Louis Minotte, of course. He's gone, Miss Killain. He's run away. I don't understand. I wanted to stop him. And you've ruined all. Let me go!"

"No! Listen to me. What was he wearing when he ran away?"

She looked at me in blank confusion.

"How should I know? Brown. Yes. A deep brown cloak against bad weather and a cowl. We all wear them in the Pennines. Against the storms, you know ..." Her eyes widened. "Yes! Like the Abbess!" She sputtered quick laughter that had no humor in it. "Why? Have you seen him? Oh, Anne!" She seized me in a grip that made me wince. "Where did he go at this hour? And why? Why?"

I shook off her hands and tried to explain, in part, what I had found in the crypt, but she was too busy over Louis Minotte to concentrate, and I decided I must show her, so instead, I told her of the watching Abbess.

"I do not know who it was watching me, Miss Amanda, but it appeared to be the creature they call the Black Abbess." She tried to interrupt, to jeer at the story of the Mist House phantom, and I knew I could not explain the monstrous thing I had suspected. Then, there was her own involvement with the dead woman. Not, of course, unless she herself had sealed the dead woman in that clay statue, and to what purpose? She had professed to like the woman. She had even suggested that Rachel Herrenrath did her spying against Lucie, thus joining Amanda's camp against the pretty widow.

"Miss Amanda, you must come with me. Something dreadful has happened in that crypt."

"Not . . . to Louis?"

I said impatiently, "No. Not to Monsieur Minotte. At least, not directly. Come along, and hurry. Do!"

She was at least accommodating enough in this that she made no more trouble and hurried along beside me. She asked several questions on the way, but I was moving too fast to answer her. The house was still silent, still dark where I had not put candles around, but I did not let myself look around into those dark and secret corners. Then, we hurried down the crypt steps and paused in the archway. I waved the candlestick for her clearer view. She gasped and then cried out, seeing only the ruin of her work.

"My statue is wrecked. Look at it. Hopeless. Who did it? Was it you?"

"Look about you," I said, motioning her farther into the crypt. "Say rather that Rachel Herrenrath wrecked your statue. And through no wish to do so. Come. Examine it."

I was myself still shaken by the diabolic horror of this business but was somewhat bolstered by the girl's own growing reaction. Her heavy features seemed weighted, somber, and ugly, but the native dignity she retained at this gruesome despoiling of her work made up for much of the almost stupid slowness of her comprehension. She finally reached the debris and stared at it.

"But why do you say Rachel did it? My work is ruined. Weeks of it. Months. I did some of it when I was too sick with the typhus even to remember."

Silently, I pointed to the uncovered portions of the face and hand and arm. She gave a quick, choking gasp and reached for the revealed flesh, then recoiled, her back striking the wall behind her.

"It . . . it is *human* beneath. Not a form—but human! Oh, God, how horrible! Horrible!"

I thought if I upbraided her in this state, she

would be the more likely to blurt out the truth.

"Miss Amanda! Look carefully at your work. Is that Mrs. Herrenrath?" As the girl continued to stare, I said sharply, "Her body as its base must have made the creation of your basic form much easier. How many other *human* bases have you used?"

She opened her mouth and whispered from dry lips, "No . . . No! You don't understand." Then, she kneeled and touched the broken bits of clay and two or three places where the flesh was revealed. She shuddered and rocked back on her heels, pleading with me. "I didn't. I swear I did not! How could I have done so?"

"Did you form this statue? Isn't it yours, Miss Dalreagh?"

She tried to glance at it but could not. I felt for emotions at this point, but my own still existed, and I knew that now, if ever, would be the only time I could get the truth from this usually strong and self-possessed girl.

"It is my work. That is, I believe so. I was at work on the base when I was taken with an infection of the lungs . . . They called it typhus, but it was not. It was Father's dying and my own stupid behavior. It rained a great deal during those days early this winter, and I walked for hours. Well," she licked her lips, sucked in deeply of the damp, fetid air, "I went to bed quite ill, though it only lasted a few days. But somehow, while I was delirious, I managed to complete most of the core, the inner form . . . At least, when I was recovering and came down to work, I found I had done considerable of it while I was sick. In fact, I had done the entire core of it, as I call the inner form."

"In short," I prompted her, "while you were too ill to know what you did, the body of this woman was covered."

We looked at each other a long, still moment. All the household sounds had ceased and our thoughts, our suspicions of what had occurred seemed to coincide in that quiet time.

"Someone else did it," she said, speaking for both of us. "Someone in Mist House completed the form while I was ill."

"And when you came back to it," I asked her, "how did you come to be convinced that you had done the work?"

I could see that she was recovering somewhat from the shock of her discovery. She put the back of her dusty hand to her forehead and thought out this disclosure.

"I suppose because no one else does this work."

"No one? In the entire household?"

She appeared to consider them one by one.

"I can't think. None of the servants, I'm certain."

"But consider the members of your family, the outsiders."

"Yes, yes. I have tried to consider. But there is no one. Uncle Richard has not done this work since his boyhood. And he is the only one . . . No! Stay! There is another." Then, she shook her head. "Absurd. Grandpapa Wye is dead."

We studied the awful remains of Mrs. Herrenrath. It was as if a broken body lay there, completely uncovered, though, of course, there was very little that we could see. But bits and bones, as it seemed, were scattered across the floor. They were the clay, the grit and sand and stone, but in these moments, they seemed to us much more sinister.

Amanda looked very sick, as, in all likelihood, I did.

"It comes to this, then," I said, trying to speak calmly, for what I had concluded was almost worse than all the rest. "The only persons with this talent who were present at the time of the housekeeper's entombment in that statue were Sir Peveril Wye and the Earl."

Amanda bit her lip and looked at me with a desperate realization.

"Anne, it cannot have been Grandpapa Wye. He was too old and not nearly strong enough. Even if there were reason or purpose in it."

"Then we are left with but one person." I

could not say his name. I cared too much. Not that one, I prayed. Please, not that one . . .

But Amanda said straight out, "Except for me, only Uncle Richard could have had the experience and the strength. But why? Anne, what will happen to us? Suppose it is Uncle, and he has run mad and did this for no purpose or some secret purpose we have not guessed. How can we stop this and protect the others? With Louis Minotte gone, we have not a man in the house except the older servants. No one but that idiot, Lucie, and you and me."

"Don't talk like this," I told her sternly, so fiercely I almost borrowed courage from it. "We know nothing of the sort. We must hope there is another explanation. In the morning, we will send to the village and to London as well for help."

"But in the meantime, think of the night we have before us!"

I was very crisp, very much the actress.

"In the meantime, we must protect ourselves!"

16

In the end, the removal of the poor creature in the crypt was left to Mrs. Kempson's son, Jeremiah, and to Amanda and me. We placed her wrapped body, together with the bits of clay and other foreign substance, in an unused cellar that was reasonably dry.

"But I tell you this to your face, mum," suggested the boy. "You'll be counting on Hobbs. He'd never go and do a thing like this. He's the man for you tonight."

Amanda shook her head.

"He's been in London since we called back Uncle for Grandfather Wye's funeral. And Uncle may be home from the village—good heavens! He may be home now. Anne, you said you saw that thing watching you. Could it have been Uncle Richard in some sort of bad weather cloak? You thought my weather cloak was a disguise for a minute or two."

"Ah no, miss!" Jeremiah cried. I could have kissed him. "His Ludship? Never! I'd sooner think it was that silly Frenchie. Beggin' yer pardon, miss," he added to Amanda.

She said nothing, but I was sure she was only practicing extreme forbearance.

We three came up out of the cellar and found ourselves shaking, now that the most repulsive task was completed.

"I'll be going back to Ma's rooms now," the boy excused himself, apologetically. "She's that feared, you've no notion."

"Of this killer?" asked Amanda, astonished. "But she knows nothing of the discovery of Rachel's body. You didn't tell her?"

"Miss Killain said I wasn't to. And I didn't. But Mama's afeared of the Abbess. The Black Abbess, that's the one to go wary of. 'Night to you, mum, and you, miss."

Amanda's head went up sharply, though she did not indicate whether she agreed or disagreed with him. But I was much disturbed.

"I hoped you might go for some sort of help, Jeremiah. We need someone here tonight. Where is the magistrate of this district? He should be fetched in as soon as possible."

"It'd take forever, mum. He's in Lincoln. Sir Jervis Grandison. And, savin' your presence, I'd be fit for Bedlam was I to go through the Dalreagh Forest tonight with the Abbess abroad."

So that ended that. Amanda began to mutter about our need for Louis Minotte, but I could not forget he had played the coward and run away. Or had he? How did one know anything for a certainty on this eery night?

We left Jeremiah, with Amanda complaining at his "cowardice," yet, I could not recall that she had made any protests beyond the suggestion about her beloved Louis Minotte. I offered to walk with her as far as her bedchamber, but she surprised me by refusing, though politely enough.

"No, Anne. I'll not ask you to do it. My staircase is close by. Yours is at the front of the house. If you go with me, you'll need to return to your own apartments in all that dark—although I am persuaded you are totally unafraid. You can't imagine her fate happening to anyone in this household. But I . . . so long as her murderer . . . or murderess is not under restraint . . ."

She started to say something pert, then was recalled to the tension of the moment, grimaced painfully, and admitted, "You are right . . . perhaps. Poor Rachel." She shuddered and gave me a little push. "Go along. I'll take these stairs. For once, I am grateful that I am on the back, not the front of the house."

"Why?" I asked, my curiosity piqued despite my worries. "Because," she called as we separated under the cloister facing the courtyard, "because, if you must know, on the front of the house you must sleep above the crypt."

I started to remind her that she spent many

of her waking hours in the crypt, but she was already gone, her heavy slippers clumping noisily up the back stairs. I crossed the courtyard, holding my arms, for it was icy cold, and the sky looked very high and very far away. There were a few scattered stars, but their distance made them seem even colder. Nor so near, nor so bright, as those in France in the precious days of my marriage.

How close I had come to allowing myself to love another man as I had my husband! It was inconceivable that Richard Dalreagh should have committed this crime. What would he gain by it? The death of an upper servant. Even if she knew too much, what could she know that would cause a man of the Earl's intelligence and character to commit such an atrocious act, totally unlike him in every respect.

Yet, what else was possible? Amanda, the girl with her very human grudges and likes? Or little Sir Percy Wye, who had once studied the art of clay-working with the young Dalreagh?

Impossible crime. Yet, it had occurred.

I stepped inside the house again but found little to comfort me there. The guardroom was big and bare and lonely. It reminded me of the night I arrived at Mist House and received that rude welcome from Amanda. But the rudeness had not been important to me because the Earl immediately came to my assistance. Now, I did not know if there would ever again be assistance for any in this unhappy household.

I took the chapel steps a minute or two later after thrusting my candle briefly into the great, vaulted room to assure myself that I would not be followed up the steps to my rooms. Nothing untoward seemed to have occurred in there since the discovery of Rachel Herrenrath's body.

As the door to my bedchamber was still locked, I went through the gallery to the sitting room, but being still fairly shaken, I glanced around into every corner before closing and bolting the door. It was exceedingly cold within the room, which surprised me, as there was a small fire glowing and snapping invitingly on the hearth. I started into the bedroom, received a blast of foggy mist, and looked back to see the portieres briskly blowing out the sitting room window. The sight was so unusual at this time of year, when the chief desire everywhere was for warmth and as few drafts as possible, that I stared at it a minute before I realized what the matter was. I stepped back to the window and examined the latch. The window could not have come open of itself. The latch was very strong. Very secure.

I looked around the room, then thought of the bedroom and glanced in again. Everything was as I had left it. Heretofore, none of the servants had entered my room in the evening after the hearth fires were seen to and my bed turned down. It was perfectly obvious, however, that someone had visited the sitting room during my absence and, for what reason I could not fathom, thrown open my sitting room window. Then, apparently being in haste, my unknown visitor hurried away without thinking to draw in the window and secure it.

While I considered this new and inexplicable mystery, I looked out of the open window before closing it and saw again what a clear view was spread before me, despite the foggy mist, of the moat bridge, the water itself, now murky in the faint light from my sitting room lamp, and the copse that marked the borders of Dalreagh Forest and the estate road to the village. Was it for some such purpose as this that my visitor had opened the window? In order to see someone or some *Thing* below on the grounds or the bridge? Very possibly.

As I drew in the window and latched it, I wondered if the creature I saw earlier watching me in the crypt had hurried up the chapel steps to this room when I went in pursuit and found only Miss Amanda instead. The sensation was an ugly one, and I turned quickly, intending to warm and cheer myself at the hearth before retiring with these fears to dog my sleep.

A jangling bell somewhere close by made me jump, and I looked into my bedchamber, noting that someone in the master apartments had summoned me. For an instant, I thought it must be Lord Richard, having returned from the village, and my heart played me false by beginning a rapid beat that proved he had not lost his appeal for me, despite the evening's events. It was not his apartment that had signaled, however, as I could see from the neatly printed little signs above the bells high on the wall. It was the apartment of Lucie Dalreagh.

I was startled enough to stare at the name above the bell for some seconds. It read "Mrs. Dalreagh," and the sign was old enough so that I knew it must refer to a Mrs. Dalreagh considerably older than Lucie . . . but I wondered if Lucie's summons would in some way refer to the peculiar running away of her worshipper, Amanda's adored Louis Minotte.

Meanwhile, I had the unpleasant task of crossing half the house at this hour not too far before midnight, and doing so in my own company, which was none too confident or secure at the moment. I took a breath, passed my hand over my windblown hair, and then went out into the passage to the Long Gallery. Nothing seemed to be stirring in the house. Even the creaking and crackling of the walls had ceased. Nonetheless, or perhaps because of this eery silence, I was intensely conscious of the darkness between each of the wall sconces and the solitary lamps I had ordered placed at what I now considered preposterous distances apart from each other.

I passed Kevin Dalreagh's room, in which I had slept on my first night at Mist House, and remembering my dead predecessor as well, I increased my steps. I was becoming surrounded by death. As I was raising my hand to knock on the door of Lucie's elaborately feminine dressing room, the door opened in my face, and blonde Phoebe peered out, her big eyes wide with fear.

"Oh, miss, I'm that glad to see you, you've no notion! We're in such trouble!" She looked up and down the dark corridor, then crooking her finger, she beckoned me into the room.

In those few seconds, I was prepared for fresh disaster, but scarcely for what Phoebe showed me, trembling all the while.

"I waited to be summoned to assist Mrs. Dalreagh for bed as always, but there was nothing. Only a few minutes ago, I came. I thought . . . I felt it was not natural. You will see, I was right."

We had come into Lucie's bedroom by this time. During the girl's nervous description, I had begun to suspect that some new truly gruesome horror awaited me, and I was therefore relieved to see that Lucie was lying in her great white testered bed with its fussy, frilled white curtains. Her eyes were closed, and it seemed perfectly obvious that she was asleep. I said as much to Phoebe.

"No, miss. Begging your pardon, but it's a bit odd about her. She just don't wake up."

I was already at the bed by this time and, looking down at the sleeping woman, called to her softly. But she slept too soundly. Phoebe's reaction had begun to disturb me. Perhaps there was a contagion in it. I shook Lucie's shoulder, trying not to hurt her or startle her, and thinking, strangely, how shocked Miss Hunnicut would be if I allowed anything to happen to her favorite "stupid" pupil. I took great care, fearing Lucie would wake up too suddenly. As I began to puzzle over her odd and hearty sleep, however, and withdrew my hand, I touched a white paper packet on the edge of her bedstand, which fell to the carpet. Absently, with a return to my normal habits, I stooped and picked up the packet, most of whose powdery contents had trickled out on the floor. The sharp edge of the little folded paper cut my fingers and I put the finger to my mouth, sucking it as I wondered what could be wrong with Lucie.

"Did you hurt yourself, miss?" Phoebe asked solicitously, and then joined me at the bedside to stare at Lucie's unconscious face.

"It was nothing. A paper cut." But there was an odd taste on my tongue, and I stared at my finger in surprise. I knew that taste. I had picked up a few grains of the powder, and they clung to my finger. Miss Hunnicut, who often had difficulty in sleeping, used the drug which she called laudanum. A large dose would not only give poor Lucie the sleep she craved, no doubt, but very possibly kill her if she were not familiar with its use. I still found it difficult to believe this was the case with her. I tasted again and then looked around the little bedstand. When I brushed against the packet of powders, I had knocked off another paper under the packet. I picked it up now, and the whole horrid business crystalized as I read the note written in Lucie's jittery hand, very like the nervous fright that was indicated in her letter to Miss Hunnicut and which had brought me up there in the first place:

> Forgive me. I should never have done the thing. But love drives us to fearful acts, and only when blood is on our hands do we know. I have sent for a runner. It is small enough payment, but it was all I could do. That, and finally to pay with my life. I am so frightened and so sorry. If it were to be done again, I would not do it, for love or for fear.
>
> Lucie Fairburn Dalreagh

"Quick!" I whispered sharply to Phoebe. "Get some water. Mrs. Dalreagh has taken a great deal of laudanum . . . by accident. We must get her on her feet and keep her up. And we must make her drink something."

The girl panicked, as I might have expected on the suggestion of poison, but in the end, she managed to locate another maid who was efficient and, fortunately, had experience with laudanum, which had been the nightly draft of her previous employer. We got Lucie to her feet, but she was completely limp and we had to bear her up for several minutes and force the water on her several times before she came around and could stand and walk of her own volition. She had not, I think, taken a deadly dose, and thus it was easier to restore her to a kind of stupified half-consciousness which was, at least, a beginning of a return to health.

I put her confession into the bodice of my gown, intending to discuss it with her later and, if the circumstances warranted, to ask the Earl's advice. It seemed to me highly improbable that Lucie had committed the crime, or crimes, at Mist House; yet, unquestionably, she was a danger to the household if she had been party to them. I could not conceive of the fussy, delicate young creature moving statues about and slapping clay over dead women. But her use of the laudanum tonight put me forcibly in mind of her husband's death. If she knew anything about the power of one drug, she might, with whatever motive, have fed her husband a drug and murdered him.

I did not pretend to fathom her reasons for the fiendish act, but quite probably such a crime, handled in her usual addlepated style, would place her open to the usages of another sort of villain, one who bled her of money or used some other power to keep her secret.

"Hello, Anne," said Lucie with a drowsy, cheerful smile.

I had been feeling a dreadful and quite unaccustomed tiredness in all my body and limbs, and when her voice told me that she would presently be her own, scatterbrained, easy self, I felt an enormous relief. I had only to put her case in hands more capable and less tired than mine. Then, I would soon be in my bed and would surely sleep until help came in the morning.

"Good evening, miss," I said, bobbing a brief curtsey.

I saw her glance around the room at the walls, where odd, tantalizing figures flickered and danced with the candlelight, and then she stared at the two maids and finally at me. She frowned.

"Send them away."

I did so, although not entirely expeditiously. I told Phoebe to wait nearby for my call. She might be required to sleep in a trundle bed in Mrs. Dalreagh's room. Shaking and uncertain, she nodded, but in spite of her fears, I saw her exchange a quick, arch glance with the other maid, and I knew the gossip of tonight's near-tragedy would soon spread over the entire house. I returned to the bedchamber.

"You wished to speak to me, Miss Lucie?"

"Oh yes. Anne? You know what happened?" She had examined the bedstand and, no doubt, guessed that I had discovered the truth of her actions. I told her I had the note and the laudanum powder, what was left of it, and I added, "There are many ways out of our difficulties, ma'am. I am persuaded yours may be resolved without—this one."

She lay back among the pillows, covering her eyes with her hands.

"Oh, God, if that were so! Don't tell anyone, will you, Anne?"

"If you will promise me not to do such a thing again. I'm sure there will be a way out. There always is."

"Perhaps. In any case—" she yawned, wriggled down under the covers, and looked at me sleepily, "I shan't do anything tonight. I daresay, what I do anyway won't matter in the least a hundred years from now."

I smiled, surprised at this cynical and philosophical outlook. It wasn't like Lucie at all.

"Very true." But meanwhile, I thought I would at least try to learn enough of the truth to brace the rest of the household against its accursed Black Abbess. "Perhaps, miss, you would be good enough to give me some hint, some warning, so that we may protect the household." It was the nearest I could come to a flat, outright question, but even this she evaded.

"Really, I . . . I wish I might help you, but I can't." She saw the change in my expression: doubt, disappointment, and, I suppose at last, suspicion. She added quickly, "I've sent Louis for the Bow Street Runners. I scraped together all the money I have for the hire of one. They're terribly capable—if you have the luck to hire a good one."

"Then you've nothing more to say to the matter?" I could not suppress the sharp edge to my voice.

She yawned again, pretended not to have heard me, and crawled down under the covers. I gave up this questioning of her for the present. The hour was late, and she had the twisting, turning agility of an eel when she chose to avoid something. I went out, leaving Phoebe to watch her, in case Lucie fell into another mood of despair and made an attempt on her life again.

Meanwhile, it seemed quite probable we must put through the rest of the night without the assistance of any competent male, and this despite the fact that one of our number actually knew the identity of Mrs. Herrenrath's murderer. I returned to my own apartment through the darkened house, making mental note to provide the corridors with taller, stouter candles. Half of them had already flickered out. The house itself, so silent earlier in the night, now drew in to its ancient walls a deep, bone-chilling cold. With it came the usual creaking sounds and then, quite suddenly, loud cracks and groans as the separate entities of Mist House first resisted and then yielded to the clammy fingers of the night.

I was running by the time I reached my sitting room. It seemed to me that even here it was much colder than it had been earlier in the evening. I went to the window to close the shutters, hoping thus to prevent the wind and fog from seeping in around the window frame. I opened the window and reached out for one of the shutters. At the same time, I saw in the distance a man on horseback, riding toward the Mist House along the estate road. I wondered if it was Richard Dalreagh and was first relieved, then troubled. Could I really take this chance with Lucie's life? If, by some dreadful fate, Richard was the murderer, then I would have shown him his danger of betrayal at Lucie's hands, and her life would be scarcely worth a farthing.

While I stared at the horseman, only faintly lighted by the luminous fog, I suddenly became aware of some movement along the forest border of the estate road. My first thought was of an animal about to scuttle across the road toward the riverbank which paralleled the road on the north side.

A few seconds later, I knew the creature hiding in the forest's shadow was a human being, very probably a man, and that he was obviously waiting there for the unsuspecting horseman. I started to call out. At the same time, the sound of hoofbeats pounded loudly through the still night air. The horseman was about to cross the moat bridge and seemed, oddly enough, headed toward the chapel and the crypt side of the building rather than the stables. Behind him, he was silently dogged by the dark-clad pursuer.

I began to recognize the form of the horseman, slim and straight, all in black, of course, as usual. He was Louis Minotte. And his pursuer? I asked myself. But I could not be sure, and I did not want to guess. I made up my mind to go out into the passage of the chapel steps without the suspicion of either of these strange beings and see if one of them betrayed his guilt—or innocence. Of one thing I could be quite certain: It was not the tutor who was following in that sinister manner. Nor had Minotte behaved in a furtive, secret way as he rode up to the house. He was the innocent one, then, and the other . . . very probably our Black Abbess.

17

I opened the passage door very slowly. Somewhat to my surprise, the hinges made no betraying sound, and I was able to move down several steps without any acknowledgment of my presence to the two men entering the chapel below. I did not know immediately, of course, that both had actually entered, though I could hear the click of riding boots on the chapel floor and assumed it was Louis Minotte. I had no notion of intruding myself on a scene of potential violence between what I supposed must be two men, for I had no weapon, although I began to wish I had a pistol of some sort, in case the tutor needed a defense.

I was on the landing where the steps turned in the opposite direction, and by leaning cautiously over the stone balustrade, I could glimpse the black-clad figure, which I took to be Louis Minotte. He had come in hurriedly, in great agitation, and then, curiously enough, called out in a low but penetrating voice, "Lucie? Where are you?" And then, as he moved about the great, hollow vault that was the chapel, "*Qui est-là? Es-tu, chérie?*"

Since I knew where Lucie was, or was presumed to be, at this moment, his question chilled me. I wondered anxiously what specific intruder he sensed as sharing the chapel with him. Surely, it must be the ominous watcher I had seen from my window. I devoutly hoped the tutor would see the creature in time to run for some help. I knew, even as I watched, that no one would come in answer to a ring from me. But I trusted lanky, brave young Jeremiah. He would come if I asked him directly, I was sure. If only Richard might be counted on!

Below me in the chapel, the tutor's heels rang on the stones of the floor as he turned abruptly. I had gone down far enough now to see him as he made a quick rush across to the altar. I watched him pause there uncertainly, look behind the altar, and then swing around toward the doorway, facing me, though as he stood in the illuminated chapel and I in the darkness of the steps, he apparently could not see me. I wondered if, perhaps, his pursuer had come into the chapel unseen by me and was still hidden from my sight, standing to one side of the archway. But no. The Frenchman saw nothing out of the ordinary, though he obviously expected to find Lucie Dalreagh somewhere in these regions. But now he was more cautious, less inclined to betray whatever private relations he shared with his dead employer's wife.

"Madame, are you here? Please to answer me. Madame? Lucie?"

He came toward the door in great haste, and in a sense, toward me. I shrank back against the wall at the turn in the steps, but I still had a clear view of the opening into the chapel and of Louis Minotte's moves. At the doorway, he peered into the dark of the steps down toward the crypt. I wondered at this morbid interest, but as I watched him closely, I noticed that some slight sound had drawn his attention to the crypt. Now, as I listened carefully, I too heard faint, betraying noises below, sounds like muffled footsteps, and hoped that he was fully aware of his danger. He put his hand to his greatcoat, and I thought he must be assuring himself that he possessed a weapon. Slightly relieved, I watched him step out on the stone landing and proceed down to the crypt.

He passed near me without apparent awareness of my presence in the dark on the lowest of the steps above the chapel. As I waited before moving beyond the chapel to the crypt steps, I pictured him passing the closet where Rachel Herrenrath's property had remained so long. It must have been he who removed the clothing, and if so, had we ever discovered his purpose in that frantic concealment?

Below me in the crypt there was suddenly a complete silence, so complete that I was made more uneasy by it than by the sound of footsteps and Minotte's voice, to which I had become accustomed. I had already started down the steps to the crypt when, from the crypt itself, came a peculiar noise I could not, for an instant, identify. A sharp intake of breath, I thought, as I came on with infinite care. The sound came again, and then Louis Minotte's voice, harsh, unlike him, still with that breathless quality which may have been horror.

"You!" Then, a pause, a choked, gasping sound, as of courage tinged with fear: "Tell me why— Let me see your face!"

Good God! What had the poor man seen, or encountered? I moved closer, so tense now I scarcely heard my own tight breathing. I could see the Frenchman standing at the north end of the crypt, his black figure looking small and slight, as if about to crumble, among those soulless, gray images of the dead. The bits and pieces of the broken statue in which we had discovered Mrs. Herrenrath were strewn around him. But I could not, at once, discover what strange being he had confronted with his anxious questions. I studied briefly each statue with its elongated, eery shadow cutting across the floor toward me.

Louis Minotte seemed to shrink back, away from the great forest of stone, and I guessed that the creature he had confronted must be hidden from me by the statues.

"The Abbess! The Abbess!" he cried, thrusting out his thin hand piteously as I, cut to the heart by that cry, turned and, careless of all betraying sounds, rushed back to the stone steps and up. The identity of the intruder had not been revealed to me after all, and I had only succeeded in bringing Louis Minotte closer to the attack and open reprisals of the deadly Abbess.

I moved as swiftly as ever in my life—yet, not fast enough, it seems. By the time I reached the chapel and was about to fling the door open into the ground-floor passage, I heard a dreadful cry, as of a man in mortal agony, and knew that the Abbess must have struck him down. I started to open the passage door and found, just when I most needed every second, that the bolt had somehow slipped over, partially locking the door. My fingers clawed at the bolt, released it finally, but not before I heard the heart-stopping sound of feet rushing up the steps from the crypt. With the utmost silence, I got the door opened and hurried down the passage. It was then, in these pools of candlelight and dark, that I heard the fluttering robes behind me and knew the ghastly truth even before I glanced over my shoulder.

The creature loomed in the darkness as an enormous, evil bird. Its wrappings, like wings, threatened to engulf the very walls in its pursuit of me. I screamed for Jeremiah and Mrs. Kempson, whose quarters were beyond the dining hall, but except for the flapping garments behind me and the rapidly pursuing feet, I heard no reply. The nightmare of my flight seemed endless.

I passed the stillroom and kitchen and hurried on to Mrs. Kempson's door, where I pounded noisily, frantically.

"Mrs. Kempson! Help me! Jeremiah! Jeremiah!"

I have no notion how long I repeated these screaming words. Not long, certainly; for the Black Abbess was gaining on me, and I had only a faint hope now, after this disturbance, of receiving help from the Kempsons in the seconds before she reached me.

I threw myself at the door and felt it reverberate under my body as I screamed again for help. Behind the door, Mrs. Kempson's sleepy voice muttered thickly, "Girl, go away! 'Tis late. And there's none here will open to the Abbess, in any case."

"The Abbess! Let me in!"

Behind the door there were muttered voices, murmurs, sharp whispers . . .

And in the passage, something reached out for me. I eluded the deadly grasp, aware of the huge, all-enveloping creature, so close around me now that I felt the frightful immediate spell of its power. I twisted, crouched away from that grasp, only just evaded it as I turned and rushed back along the corridor past the first dining hall door, which was ajar.

It was excessively dark there in the shadowy space between two low-burning tapers, and I ran desperately through the dining hall, though without hope of throwing off that ominous pursuer, so like death itself. It may have been the darkness or simply that I had run faster and more silently than I thought, but once I was hurrying along one side of the great, empty hall, I heard no following footsteps. I dared not hope I had fooled the Abbess; yet, no one was behind me. I was running fairly near the long table—which had not yet been set back.

As I moved around chairs and sideboards, something flashed on the carpet scarcely a hair's breadth beyond my hurrying steps. I reached down and clutched a silver dinner knife tight in my fingers. It might not be the strongest weapon in the world, but it was better than nothing.

I paused at last, at the far end of the dining hall by the open door into the passage. My heart was pounding so loudly against my breastbone I felt sure the Abbess must hear it. But the long passage, its deadly dark now a blessing to me, appeared empty. As I stepped into the hall again, I took care not to present a silhouette against the faint light that drifted into the dining hall from the high east windows. I knew that if I could possibly have thrown off my silent, murderous pursuer, I must see to Louis Minotte. Since there had been no sight nor sound from him during my futile run for help, he was probably unconscious, or even dead. Someone had to bring help to this wretched household, gripped now in the power of this maniacal Abbess.

It would be bitter cold outside, and I, though warmly enough dressed for bed, was in no case to leave Mist House at this hour of the night. The only hope, the only sensible thing left for me, was to return to my rooms and bolt myself in until dawn. I got as far as the chapel steps below my rooms when I heard faint but betraying sounds over my head on the flight of steps between me and the housekeeper's quarters. The Abbess would be waiting for me!

Frantic now, too exhausted after my recent exertions to feel capable of a vigorous defense, I backed away from those sounds, and fumbling behind me for the stone balustrade, made my way back down the crypt steps, one by one.

Where is Richard? I thought in tired despair. Was there no help to count on? None but Louis Minotte. A slender reed, at best, and now, as I stumbled down into the crypt, I saw by the flickering light that he was not even that. He lay crumpled on the broken pieces of clay that had once so horribly encased the remains of the murdered Rachel Herrenrath.

But as I stumbled to his side, I saw with enormous relief that the French tutor still breathed. Before touching him, I listened carefully but heard nothing more abovestairs. Perhaps the creature who haunted this house in a very real and bloodthirsty manner had now retreated to whatever lair concealed it after its forays.

I crouched before him, turning his body over with fingers as gentle as possible, though they still shook from my recent close escape and must have been a frightful chill on the poor man's flesh, for they felt freezing cold, even to me. I could have borne with the sight of blood, the use of a weapon by his attacker, the Abbess, but this—mere hands had apparently attacked the unfortunate young tutor. He showed every sign of attempted strangulation. A hideous sight and one which I had seen but once before.

Minutes must have passed while I ministered to the Frenchman, but as he seemed to come around, and my fingers thawed, I wondered if we were to have a few hours of calm after the recent nightmare.

"Lucie," murmured the poor, besotted man; he had come so close to death and yet still thought only of his beloved.

"No, monsieur," I corrected him softly, and

added in French, "We are in much danger. The Abbess may hear us. Have a care, monsieur."

"Lucie . . ." murmured the young man, gazing at me out of glazed eyes. It was still difficult for him to speak. He was hoarse, and his tongue was swollen. But I would not have minded this, would even have encouraged it, except for the danger. I doubted if his voice could be heard beyond the crypt, but there was still the possibility, the monstrous possibility that the creature was still hanging about.

"Can you walk? We must get to safety. Lock ourselves in."

"I'll . . . try." With his help, I managed to get him to his knees, but no further. He seemed to stare through and beyond me in the direction of the archway. It was unnerving to have him stare at empty space behind my back.

"The Abbess!" he whispered, the pupils of his eyes dilated, his gaze disoriented.

"Yes, yes. I know," I whispered, trying to hold him upright. "Did you discover who it really is?"

He seemed to shrink within himself, scrambling furtively to get behind me.

"The Abbess!"

Even then, I scarcely believed the hideous thing he tried to tell me until I had twisted around to see what attracted his peculiar stare. The great creature loomed there in the archway, a massive, blurred thing, now corporeal, now phantom, while the taper flickered lower and lower. It was motionless; yet, I could see the eyes gleaming terribly as they caught the light.

"Please—leave us . . ." I whispered, staring at the strange, surely subhuman creature. "He is hurt. Don't you see?"

The Thing moved ever so slowly, and again I had the sense of being engulfed, eaten, totally held by this huge, shadowy thing so like black death. I was confused by those eyes gleaming out of the Abbess' cowl and by their endless repetition in all the gray-clad nuns that stood about us casting their elongated shadows. I felt the curious sensation that the Abbess was one of those stone images until I became aware that the Abbess had moved again. We are done for now, I thought . . .

Louis Minotte cried out weakly, warding off the sight, and I tried to interpose my body between the weakened man and the sight that aroused his terror even more than my own. As I leaned over the tutor, I found beneath him the table knife; I had dropped it. Even in our extremity of terror, I remembered now the revival of my courage at the touch of that cold metal when my fingers closed on it.

But the glistening eyes within that hood missed nothing. As I tried to raise my hand to a level where I might conceal the knife in my robe, it leaped at the half-conscious tutor and at me. The cowl of its all-encompassing robe slipped back, so that as I crouched away from his terrible hands, I saw the features revealed in the taper light—Richard Dalreagh's features, but features distorted, exaggerated, in every way a caricature of the face I had learned to love. So shocked was I at this that when his deadly hands clawed for my throat, I could scarcely scream, and the poor weapon I had I now held as weakly as a small child. My shock, and my horror at this revelation were so great that the defense of my own life was made more difficult. I tried to say his name: "Richard . . . please . . . Richard . . ." But the monstrous nightmare muted my cry, and when the voice spoke, the sound was blurred and strange, not like Richard at all.

"You let him take Lucie—that unutterable person—take my wife . . ."

I screamed, shrilly, not understanding, thinking Richard had gone mad to be speaking so. And then, as I tried to drag myself away from him, those great fingers encircled my head, and I cried out again, one sound, a strangled noise, barely evading his grasp, imagining still that I heard the "Abbess" abovestairs, the footsteps approaching. Then he had tightened his grasp on my throat, and only my dimming consciousness imagined Richard in two places at once.

I remember that my hand with the dinner knife made some vain, tentative effort at a thrust, and then, the scene began to fade before my eyes. There was a terrible pressure against my throat, and my breath was cut off. The monstrous distortion of the face I had loved swam before my eyes.

And then—furious sounds. A confusion I could not see nor identify.

"Richard!" It was my voice, but harsh, breathless. I felt myself drifting into unconsciousness, into rest. Something struck hard against me, and the pressure ceased, and vaguely, I realized Louis Minotte had tried to defend me, falling on my body to offer his poor protection. Now, together, we watched the incredible scene: for the Abbess, whose face had seemed a caricature of our own Richard Dalreagh, suddenly confronted a cloaked and booted man in the archway and this newcomer was surely the Earl of Dalreagh. What, then, was the monster whose strength and brutality had sent this household into such terror?

The real Richard Dalreagh did not seem to be armed, and I was terrified for him as he moved forward rapidly, leaped, as it seemed, to the creature as like him as a crude drawing is like to its original. Seeing that the "Abbess" had raised my table knife, which gleamed sharply, and that Lord Richard threw himself against it, I cried out again and struggled to help him, but Louis Minotte kept me back.

"Who is it?" I asked, confused and sickened at what looked to be the beginning of a bloody conflict.

"It is poor Lucie's secret, I fear," the tutor told me. "The—the Abbess is her late husband, Kevin. Not quite as late as he was thought to be," he ended with what I considered a typical misplaced French irony.

"But good God! He was dead!"

Louis Minotte shook his head. "She loved him very much. She has never denied that, and she saw him going mad before her eyes. Then, there was the disappearance of the housekeeper, Madame Herrenrath . . . In any case, Lucie chose to try and prevent her husband's being removed to the horrors of Bedlam. And for all my own adoration of that sweet, that incomparable little woman, I have always known she was deeply devoted to her husband. When she asked my help, I could do no more than oblige her. Adorable creature, so intensely loyal!"

"Don't!" I whispered. "We must help the Earl. We must—"

But we saw that it was too late, even as I dragged myself away from the Frenchman's grasp and tried to seize the arm of the "Abbess" Kevin Dalreagh. I got no further. Richard struck swiftly and hard with the edge of his open hand, and his brother, clawing at his own throat, stumbled, then fell, only just missing the Frenchman and me.

The terror and the anguish of the moment was accentuated by an ear-piercing female scream, and the words, "Father! Father!" as young Amanda Dalreagh rushed into the room to kneel before her father. Richard shook the man very slightly by the shoulder. I could see the terrible concern in his face, as in Amanda's, and despite my own close escape from the hands of the masquerading Kevin Dalreagh, I felt deeply the suffering of the two who knelt over the fallen man at this minute.

"Kevin . . . lad," murmured Richard in a voice whose poignant sadness made tears start in my eyes.

Louis Minotte, too, was touched—more, I think on Amanda's account than that of the Earl—but he looked up from the fallen man in the dark dressing gown so like a nun's habit and said softly, "I fear your brother is dead, Your Lordship. The blow knocked his head against the corner at the base of this statue . . . I regret . . ."

Amanda was crying now, and the Frenchman put his arm out, tentatively, around her shoulder.

I myself did not regret the passing of the dead creature, but my sympathy with our rescuer was no less powerful.

"And you, dearest Anne?" Richard asked in

that voice so unusual to his proud nature, yet so endearing.

I put my hand in his outstretched fingers. His hand was still shaking a little. Then, it steadied. My own hand felt secure in his strength. We heard nothing now except the sobbing of the now truly twice bereaved Amanda.

18

And then, at last, it was day—an extraordinarily sunny one for winter, a day that I had, at one time, despaired of ever seeing again.

Richard did not summon me to Lucie Dalreagh's sitting room until late in the morning, for he thought, as he told me later, that I would need rest after the terrible night. But the truth is that I had been unable to remain in bed. It seemed to me that I could best banish my frightful memories by hard work. Amanda Dalreagh found me first where, at the moment, I was most content to be, in the dining hall, polishing the heavily carved sideboard.

"Good heavens, Miss Killain! Does nothing disturb you?" she asked in a not too pleasant voice.

She had wept in the night, and her eyes bore the faint signs of her second farewell to the body of her father, but otherwise, the girl was very much her reserved and carefully controlled self. She picked up the bundle of broomstraws abandoned by a parlor maid who had been summoned by Mrs. Kempson, and while I was wondering what the daughter of the great House of Dalreagh could possibly find to do with broom-straws, she set to work briskly sweeping the floor. As she approached me, she said flatly, "I consider that Papa died weeks ago and that anything which may have been done since . . . any so-called crime, that is to say, was the fault of . . . of someone who did not have my father's mind or his soul."

"Quite true, miss. I am of that belief myself," I said honestly. I might feel that Kevin Dalreagh should have been put away in Bedlam, despite the notoriously shocking conditions in that madhouse, but I could scarcely tell his daughter so.

We worked silently a few minutes, and then Amanda said, as though I had not been arguing the matter, "I should have guessed. No! I really *should* have guessed. Father was better than Uncle Richard with the clay and the sculpting. Only Father or I could have concealed Rachel Herrenrath so skillfully."

I would scarcely admire the fiendish business, but otherwise, I could only agree with the girl, adding, "Mrs. Dalreagh—that is to say, your stepmother—mentioned your father's having been injured when thrown from his horse last autumn. His Lordship once told me he had asked your father to see a surgeon about his headaches. I daresay that fall was the cause of it all."

She said quickly, "Yes. I knew. He acted so very—odd. Cruel and bad-tempered. Horrid sometimes. He struck Lucie. And he began to hate Rachel. I remember now. He said she was forever spying on him. He began to take the poor woman in the strongest dislike. But Anne, if you could have known Father before! He was always quick of temper, but so dear. Ever so funny and nice. A jolly person." Her voice broke, and I looked away, much moved by the emotion which she suppressed almost at once.

We were completing the work in the dining hall when the Earl spoke to us.

"Good Lord! Have either of you managed to get any rest? Amanda, what are you doing on your hands and knees? Anne, will you and my niece come up with me to Lucie's sitting room?"

I smiled at him, but I suppose I did not move rapidly enough in dropping the dusting cloth, because he strode across the floor and impolitely snatched the cloth from my hand. Though he was himself to me, courteous and even solicitous in his brisk way, there were still the marks of the previous night's horror in his eyes and in the faint lines of his face. As the three of us went up the back stairs, with Amanda going several steps before us, he asked me suddenly, excluding his own natural feelings from the question, "Had you any knowledge that my brother lived?"

"None, sir." He smiled faintly at the "sir," and I wondered that I should ever have thought him excessively proud or haughty.

"In any case, my dear Anne, the pain of the recent events is considerably softened."

I was puzzled at this remark and fell into the warm and charming trap he had laid for me.

"Softened how, my Lord?"

"Because Lucie's secret, her effort to preserve and cure my poor brother, has brought Miss Anne Killain to Mist House."

I flushed with pleasure and yet was ashamed that I could feel pleasure in such a time of pain for the Dalreaghs.

By the time we reached the upper stories of Mist House, we were hard put to avoid the strange men I saw stalking about, two of them carrying bits of paper on which many notes had been penned.

"Two are from the constable at Lincoln, and the other, the little man, is the fellow I sent for at the headquarters of the Bow Street Runners in London," said the Earl. "Minotte set out for the Runners last night, you know, and then could not leave Lucie to whatever dangers she faced here, and he returned. However, the investigation seems to have terminated rather quickly, I am happy to say. I imagine they must have spoken with my sister-in-law."

"She should have told you," Amanda grumbled ahead of us. "I would have helped her. I would never have let Father be taken off to Bedlam. No need for her elaborate pretense that he was dead when he was not."

Richard tightened his grasp on my arm as he said, carefully excluding emotion, "That is foolish talk, Amanda. By her pretense, and by not having my brother restrained, Lucie certainly brought about Peveril's death." He looked at me, hesitated, then added, having thought it over, "But it is no fault of hers. I should have guessed his condition. I was so busy with my precious bill in Parliament."

"You were not at Mist House when your brother died? That is," I amended, considering the incredible situation I had stumbled on, "when he appeared to die?"

He paused, but only an instant, as he gestured that I should go before him along the corridor. "No. I was not here. I did not even see poor Kevin before she had him in his coffin—as I thought. I was in London, pursuing the passage of this bill. Well, no matter now. I was not here when I was needed. Poor, frail Lucie! She did all to preserve my brother. All!"

We were passing the door to Lucie Dalreagh's apartment when I stopped, and the Earl, perhaps with other weighty matters on his mind, stopped afterward and reached over my head to push open the door.

Lucie Dalreagh appeared to be holding court, for she sat up in her bed, propped by pillows, another of which the Frenchman was adding to the collection. Like me, the Frenchman looked battered and bruised about the face, his white cravat concealed the marks on his throat, but if he had been Lucie's assistant in clearing away the ravages made by the madman's occasional forays, I could well understand the serenity now in his face, despite last night's injuries.

Amanda sat stiffly on a little footstool below the bed, her arms clasped around her knees. I suspected, from the way she watched her stepmother and Louis Minotte without malice, that she had resigned herself to the romance in this quarter. I had my own assumption about Lucie's kindness to her late husband. Undoubtedly, there was in it some feeling of guilt as she was drawn closer to Minotte while her mad husband displayed more and more criminal tendencies. The very fact that she discovered in herself some predilection for Louis Minotte would make her work harder to preserve Kevin Dalreagh from the horrors of Bedlam.

"Well now, let us have your story, my dear Lucie," said Richard, bringing forward a chair for me and standing behind it with his hand on my shoulder in a proprietary way that I liked.

Lucie, looking smaller, more wan and frail than ever among all those pillows, protested weakly, "I never meant it to go so far. I thought he would come out of his last rages, when poor

Rachel disappeared. I suspected—but I did not know. And Kevin had always been so good to me. Until his hunting accident. I thought if he remained in the cellar rooms, with the door locked, then when he came to himself, I could let him out, and we would tell the world how he had been cured."

"I still don't know why you didn't tell me of your fears and of his madness," Richard put in. "I suppose you must have given him laudanum or some such drug to simulate death."

Amanda looked up. "I saw Father on his deathbed for a moment. At least, I thought he was dead. I did not stay."

"Don't you see?" Lucie explained, wringing her thin hands. "You Dalreaghs are strong. Ruthless. You'd have had poor Kevin put to that place."

"What place?" asked Richard, beginning to frown.

"She means Bedlam, Uncle. And very probably she is right."

"Very probably," he agreed, "for the safety of the household." And Lucie shuddered.

"When I was a child, I was taken to Bedlam to watch the antics of those poor creatures. I remember how my brothers and my father laughed. It was great sport to watch those mad things tearing at their chains, and moaning, and—"

"Don't!" cried Amanda, hoarsely, and added, "I only wish you had trusted me to help you."

But Richard pursued the main thread of Lucie's story.

"How did you get my brother down to the cellars? He is a big man."

Louis Minotte agreed with a reminiscent grimace.

"We had to wait until deep in the night. We half-carried, half-dragged him. And then, he was beginning to regain consciousness. It—it was not easy."

I could well imagine, and I wondered at the spell cast by the supposedly helpless and weak Lucie Fairburn whom I had known at Miss Hunnicut's School. It was quite plain, however, that the Frenchman did not regret a single action he had performed in the service of his idol.

"Then," she went on sadly, "Poor Kevin began to imagine Louis was my lover and that we were putting him out of our way, locking him into that room for our own purposes. Somehow, he managed to get out, several times. I daresay one key fits most of the locks here in this wretched house."

"Excuse me," I said, interrupting the recitation of this family tragedy for the first time. "What was the immediate act that made you decide you must have Mister Kevin put under restraint?"

Lucie sighed. "When Mrs. Herrenrath did not appear for an entire day and night. It was at the same time that Amanda became ill. And when Rachel did not come for her property, I suspected . . ."

"I left my statue unfinished," the girl explained to us. "And of course, now I see that Father must have completed it and, incidentally, have concealed Rachel within."

Lucie covered her ears.

"Don't. I was sure Kevin must have caught her watching him one night and killed her. And I knew then that he must be put under restraint. But neither Louis nor I could imagine what he had done with the . . . body. It was then I told Louis how I wished to keep Kevin safe from Bedlam and at the same time prevent his harming anyone else." She lowered her hands, and stared into space. "There were times, even after we got him locked into that room, when I would visit him and he was himself, dear and kind. He thanked me for what I had done. You see, he understood at those times how dangerous it might be if he were permitted to remain free. But toward the last . . . it was nearly worth my life to enter. He was so fierce, so unlike himself."

Richard moved to the bedside and, for the first time, looked at Lucie with the respect she deserved for her brave, if ill-advised, attempt to protect her husband.

"It is obvious now what Peveril saw that night in the chapel. The sight of a man whose burial he had supposedly witnessed might be enough to jar the sensibilities of a much younger person. It was criminal folly, my dear Lucie. But I know why you tried to protect Kevin from Bedlam. I, too, have seen that place." He shook his head at his own words as he ended, "And while I was busy trying to pass laws for the improvement of conditions in England, you were doing something material about it. Have you told the constable's men the true tale?"

She shrugged. "Only so much as they had to know. They examined Kevin's . . . body, so they guessed the rest."

Richard nodded. "I shall make a complete report myself. Perhaps, my poor brother may not have suffered vainly, if this can influence the passage of a bill for the treatment of such cases. Now, Lucie, we will leave you to rest for a time."

We all left the room, except Louis Minotte, who once more plumped up the pillows behind her, and I was greatly relieved to notice that Amanda paid him scant attention. As the three of us went toward the front of the house, Amanda said suddenly, "I daresay this secret explains why the poor creature walked in her sleep. It was a dreadful thing to have on one's conscience." She sighed, adding unsteadily, "In the circumstances, I am glad Papa . . . is gone."

"Yes," Richard told her in the gentle way that was so rare, and so much more treasured in him because of its rarity. "It is better. The dear chap we knew died when that injury overcame him. We must think of it in that way."

When Amanda left us, after a glance at her uncle's face and then at mine, I said hastily, "I understand why Lucie wanted me to come to Mist House after the other housekeeper's disappearance. She felt that I would be discreet, having been her friend in former days."

"Probably." He was looking at me in a way that made me deeply aware of the unacknowledged feelings between us. I tried to think of something to say, to bridge the awkward gap, but he cut me short by taking my shoulders in the tight grasp of his two hands.

"You are about to say your work here is done and that you must move on; isn't it so?" Before I could agree, he continued. "That may be. And if it is, then when I kiss you, you must regard yourself as my equal, not my employee, and any act between us is that of a man to his affianced wife." He shook me a little. "Is that clear?"

"I cannot say," I told him gravely. "I must judge by the . . . act."

But very soon I was enabled to judge, for myself, and so I did. He had made it perfectly clear and had told me the truth.